VIGGO THE OBSESSION

A WOLF SHIFTER FATED MATES PARANORMAL ROMANCE

BILLIONAIRE WOLVES SERIES
BOOK FOUR

CHARMAINE LOUISE SHELTON

CONTENTS

WANT FREE BOOKS?

Want to know what happened to Jagger's best friend Dylan? Find out in *Dylan The Rogue: A Wolf Shifter Fated Mates Paranormal Romance* **your FREE Book!**

Click Cover Below or visit **bit.ly/ CLBooksDylanTheRogue** to subscribe to my newsletter for latest news and launches, books from my author friends, and sizzling reads in book promotions. Plus, start reading the steamy fated mates romance for bad boy wolf shifter Dylan.

ABOUT VIGGO THE OBSESSION: A WOLF SHIFTER FATED MATES PARANORMAL ROMANCE

I'm the playboy prince who vowed it would never happen. Then it did. And she became my obsession.

Every female, she-wolf and human, wants a piece of me. So why should I choose only one? Unlike my brother—the leader of our pack, the Billionaire Wolves of Miami—and our best friends, I have zero interest in settling down with my fated mate. If she even exists.

But then Maya Alejandra Perez Garcia walks into my club.

I love the life I made for myself in Miami, away from my controlling family in Venezuela. They allow me to leave until I turn twenty-five. Now, they demand I return to marry a man of their choosing, not mine. Before I go, I have one night to do as my heart wants. And it's Viggo

Larson, the sexy as sin man who watches me with smoldering eyes.

How could I know my steamy act of rebellion would result in a surprise and Viggo having one of his own?

*Their steamy love story is a standalone in the sizzling **Billionaire Wolves Series** of interconnecting stories featuring wolf shifter fated mates romance. Get a glimpse of their dynamism in other books.*

Anthem: "She Bangs" Ricky Martin
https://www.youtube.com/watch?v=5ihtX86JzmA

Visit CharmaineLouiseBooks.com

CHAPTER 1

 iggo

I vow to not end up like the others.

No.

You won't catch this billionaire playboy prince of the pack chasing after his fated mate. Facing death to save her. Being rejected. Losing all control. In front of humans, no less.

Not this wolf shifter.

Although I would risk all to save my fated mate. If I had one. Which I don't. And have no interest in one at the moment.

As the youngest at twenty-eight of my best friends—including my older brother by two years, Jagger Larson, our pack's Alpha—the single life suits me just fine. A plethora of females—she-wolf and human—want a piece of me. So why choose only one? I can have the pick of the pack, no pun.

Plus, my work as the President of Clubs and Lounges for Larson Enterprises, Inc. keeps me busy and out with late nights several times a week. It's our family's multibillion-dollar company founded in Miami with Jagger as the current CEO. We're the top company in the hospitality industry for luxury hotels, fine dining, clubs, and lounges.

Initially, Jagger was hesitant to select me to run the clubs and lounges. I persuaded him I could handle the role because of my years of not only hanging out at them but also managing a few. The hot and happening Miami nightlife is right in my wheelhouse.

He relented to a trial, and I give it my all. My division generates a sizable amount of revenue each year. Now, Jagger admits his fun-loving and smart brother increases overall profits for Larson Enterprises regularly.

But it's not enough.

I want to shed the perception as the younger brother who makes his way on the back of the pack Alpha and as the carefree jokester with the loftiest achievement of banging multiple females in a night. No. My goal is to prove I'm my own male to be taken seriously. I won't become a boring bump on a log. But others will view me as responsible and respected.

Which is the reason I'm slogging through quarterly numbers with the CFO—a member of our pack—instead of joining Jagger and our best friends for a night at Club

Hati. Tag Dahl—the pack beta and COO of Larson Enterprises—called earlier to tell me about the plan to hang out. Normally, I would be all on it. However, two things stopped me. My division numbers' projections are lower than expected and me being the ninth wheel.

Tag is the most recent of the five of us to meet his fated mate Wren Byrd. Jagger was the first to leave bachelorhood when he found Sasha Waters—the High Witch and the leader of her coven—again. Dylan Vang, the rogue wolf who didn't even believe in fated mates, fell hard for Sasha Volkov. Rust Ingolf—our pack doctor—overcame the rejection of Natalie Moore to claim her as his fated mate.

Which leaves me… The last male standing.

So, as much as a night of partying with my buddies appeals to me, joining them with their females dulls my enthusiasm. Not that I don't like them. They're my new sisters added to my actual younger one, Signy. However, I'd rather study spreadsheets until my eyeballs fall out than to witness powerful wolf shifters going gaga over their females and I don't have one. Again, not that I want one. So, no thanks.

I told Tag as much. Of course, he ribbed me and said he couldn't wait for me to meet my match. I ended the call with him guffawing.

"All right, Viggo. This explains the difference in the numbers. Here, look at this column…"

The CFO shares his laptop's screen to the television mounted on the wall across from the conference table in my office on the executive floor of The Larson Tower.

I scrub a hand over my exhausted ice blue eyes and swipe it through the longer top strands of my fiery copper red hair. Determined to find the cause, I focus on the detailed spreadsheet. An hour later, I unfold my muscular frame and stretch all six feet, six inches with a groan. Then thank the CFO for staying late. We part ways in the garage.

The engine of my Ferrari 488 Pista purrs to life. As I maneuver the streets of Downtown Miami Bayfront, headed for my beachfront penthouse on Ocean Drive, I decide to swing by Club Hati. After hours of numbers, I can use a drink and the distraction of a female—or two.

The supercar stops in front of an Art Deco building in a prime spot on Ocean Drive that offers unobstructed views of the Atlantic Ocean. The building stands three stories with a rooftop lounge and has a sleek linear appearance with stylized ornamentation. A sectioned-off outdoor area offers seating for dining and drinking at the bar.

Two males in custom-tailored black suits flank the entry. A queue extends around the corner of people in expensive attire patiently awaiting admittance to the club. Not surprising given Club Hati is for the über-wealthy and influential, too refined to behave boorishly. The hopeful patrons are not rambunctious as one would ordinarily see waiting outside a South Beach nightclub.

I chose Club Hati for the name as a nod to Norse mythology. The wolf Hati chases the moon across the night sky. His counterpart—the wolf Sköll—chases the sun during the day. They do so until the time of Ragnarök when they will swallow the heavenly bodies.

A valet waits for me to emerge.

"Good evening, Mr. Larson," he says as he bows his head respectfully.

He and the doorman are members of our pack. Enforcers who are perfect to handle any issues at the club should they arise.

I enter the club where the air vibrates with the pulse of the music. The scent of expensive perfume and cologne mixes with an enticing aroma the club pumps through the ventilation system. Colorful lights change periodically.

My gaze roams around the lavish club full of the glitterati. Celebrities, socialites, fashionistas, and billionaire tycoons wear their sexiest, most revealing outfits. With my enhanced senses, I distinguish wolf shifters from humans easily. Bottles of top-shelf liquor and magnums of champagne sit atop the tables in the VIP booths. Assigned female servers in figure-fitting white tube mini dresses carry bottles with sparklers. The patrons applaud.

Those not fortunate to have a booth stand two deep at the three bars or perch on stools at high-top tables surrounding the dance floor. Bartenders stay busy serving drinks to those gathered.

The dance floor teems with gyrating bodies. Females dressed in revealing outfits dance with metrosexual males and macho types. Partiers shake their asses in hopes of hookups.

Pride fills my chest as I weave through the crowd—a head above most others—bound for my office. With floor-to-ceiling windows perched above the dance floor, my office offers the perfect spot to survey the activities.

In addition to employing wolf shifters and humans, Larson Enterprises' establishments cater to both. Best for our kind to hide in plain sight and all. Although we've been here a hell of a lot longer than the humans.

Several millennia ago, Scandinavian Viking wolf shifters sailed from the Old World and landed along the East Coast of what's now the United States. The six packs headed by best friends who sought new lands moved throughout the continent to form territories, with ours settling here. We maintain close ties with our brethren through friendship, mating, and business. Plus, our Ruling Council gatherings keep us informed of happenings throughout the packs.

Our Miami Wolves Pack is the most powerful pack in the South. Because of the success of Larson Enterprises, other packs refer to us as the *Billionaire Wolves of Miami*. Further reason for me to ensure I succeed in my responsibility to generate revenue through my division.

With a nod at the security guard standing at the foot of the staircase leading to my office, I jog up the steps. Once inside, I make a beeline for the wet bar in the corner. Crystal decanters filled with clear and amber liquids glow in the low lights. Striding towards the wall of one-way windows, I sip on Scotch as I watch the happenings below. Then notice my brother and best friends with their fated mates in the VIP section.

They're clustered together on white leather banquettes

with their drinks on low tables in front of them. Their faces radiate with the happiness of true love.

For a moment, a twinge zaps my heart. What would it be like to have a partner the gods choose for me as The One? A she-wolf who senses my needs and my emotions through our bond? Who will spend the rest of her life with me and bear my pups?

Nah!

I shake my head to dislodge the slipup and toss back the rest of my drink.

Wren leads the females to the dance floor. She's the first human turned into a she-wolf by a male wolf shifter in our pack in decades. Thankfully for Tag, she had a successful full transition. Some humans die. Others cannot shift but live longer with better health. The pack treats all turned she-wolves equal to those born as wolf shifters. Then there's the mental aspect of it all. It's a lot for the mind to process the concept of being a wolf shifter.

I don't know if I could handle waiting to see if a human mate will survive my claiming bite. Normally, a male wolf shifter issues it to lodge his scent via a serum in a she-wolf's skin permanently marking her as his mate. The scent wards off other males. Once issued, the pair can never part or the male wolf shifter will go crazy and lose control of his wolf.

However, the claiming bite is also the only way to turn a human female into a she-wolf. The serum enacts the transformation. The process can last for days while she remains in a coma to allow her body to change on a cellular level. A deep sleep they may or may not awake from. And if they do, will they maintain their sanity?

A shudder runs through me.

I pivot and stride to the bar to refill my drink.

Back at the glass wall, I scan the crowded dance floor. The DJ has the partiers gyrating to the slamming music. Even though it's muffled by the wall, the sound reaches my ears easily.

The DJ is an upcoming local favorite. I like to give people in the community opportunities to excel as Jagger did for me. I make a mental note to tell the club's manager to schedule the DJ for a few more nights this month. If he keeps packing the dance floor, we'll put him on the regular rotation.

My head bops to the beat as I gaze at the DJ. Then it snaps to a stunningly beautiful female on a platform next to his booth. Lost in her own world, she has her eyes closed and moves seductively to the beat.

Glossy jet black hair sways to brush her round ass. And that's only the beginning of her curvy, tight body. Bountiful tits—almost too full for my sizable hands to cover— play peekaboo from behind the deep v-neckline of her silver mini dress. Tiny crystals dangle from it and shimmer with each shake of her grip-worthy hips that flow out from a narrow waist. Long, toned golden legs end in sky-high, fuck-me strappy sandals. More crystals dazzle as her feet glide across the floor in time with the beat.

My cock punches a hole in my bespoke suit trousers.

Mesmerized, I watch the female.

Then Wren appears and throws her arms around the beauty's neck for a hug before she introduces her to the others. The beauty grins and hugs them too. Even from this distance, her expressive topaz eyes glitter more than the sparkling crystals that adorn her sinful body. She saunters to the DJ and whispers in his ear.

Jealousy unfurls hot in my chest. The visceral reaction surprises me. I watch as he nods, and she returns to Wren.

When the music blends to T.I.'s "Live Your Life," they embrace again. The beauty's hips sway as they dance and sing. She spins as she throws her hands up and shakes her mouth-watering ass. The hem of her mini dress rises to expose more of her golden skin. She twirls and bumps a hip against Wren's. The beauty giggles and shimmies some more, hypnotizing me with her seductive spell.

Fuck. Me.

Inexplicably drawn to her like a moth to a flame, my feet lead me from the office, down the stairs, and into the shadows near the DJ booth. This close, her beauty surpasses that of any female I've ever seen. Her eyes hooded, golden cheeks flushed, and lush mouth curled up make me wonder what she'd look like as I brought her to a screaming climax on my impressive cock.

It thumps along my thigh, eager to make the fantasy a reality. The heel of my palm strokes down against its length to soothe the burning ache of instant desire. A throaty growl slips from my mouth.

Then my nostrils flare.

A whiff of my first breath as a newborn pup slams into

my system. The unique scent of fragrant frangipani mixed with fresh coconuts and salt carried on a tropical breeze from the Caribbean Sea fills my lungs anew. It triggers an ancient and unstoppable chain reaction.

An electric current weaves its way to zap my brain, alerting my entire body to a specific presence. Eyes flash silver with my wolf as enhanced vision zooms around the club and my head tilts back on a deep inhalation to pinpoint the location. Heartbeat speeds up faster than the Ferrari going from 0 to 100 in 2.9 seconds. My cock pulses with the pounding rhythm as it grows diamond hard and pre-cum oozes from the tip.

My wolf claws at my skin to break free for the carnal hunt.

I all but throw my head back and howl like a feral beast maddened by lust and the urge to claim. To possess. To breed.

My fated mate.

She's here.

And I will have her.

Now.

Or tear this club apart.

Nothing and no one will keep her from me.

MINE.

CHAPTER 2

aya

THE TROPICAL SUN warms my skin as I hike along the steep trail in Waraira Repano National Park on the edge of Caracas. My golden skin glistens from a sheen of sweat. Thighs and calves burn from the two-hour climb to the hidden waterfall. Beneath the tank top, sweat trickles down my spine to the waistband of my cargo shorts. I adjust the straps on the backpack as it slips from my damp shoulders, then swipe a loose strand of hair from my brow.

Ahead, the trail widens as the trees separate. The sound of rushing water overtakes the cries of querrequerre birds and the scurrying of small animals in the undergrowth. All indicate my arrival at the base of the waterfall. The water cascades over the cliff to form a crystal-clear pool. Its surface dappled by the sunlight promises a refreshing reprieve from the heat.

I grin at the sight of it as my pace quickens to reach my goal. A glance around confirms no other in the vicinity. Only a few colorful butterflies flitter amongst the abundant flowers around the edge. The surrounding grass empty. All alone. Perfect for me to skinny-dip.

With a whoop, I shrug my backpack off and drop it to the ground. Crouching, I untie my boots then remove them, flexing my toes as they emerge from thick wool socks. I stand and shimmy out of the shorts and hipster briefs before I yank my tank and sports bra off. The clothes land in a pile on the backpack as I remove the hair tie and shake my head. The tips of my jet black hair tickle the curve of my butt.

My head tilts back as I raise my arms, fingers spread to the cerulean blue, cloudless sky to bask in the sun. A deep inhalation expands my chest. Brown beaded nipples point towards the sky as I bend backwards and rise to my toes for a much-needed stretch. On an exhalation, I straighten and dash into the natural pool.

A squeal pops from my mouth as the unexpected chill of the water sluices over my heated skin. I take a deep breath and plunge beneath its surface. Tapping into my inner Ariel, I press my legs together and flick them like a tail as my arms propel me forward. I swim a few laps as I luxuriate in the tranquility of the tucked-away jewel of the park. As I float on my back, I close my eyes and let go.

The hairs on the back of my neck rise. The tingling

sensation of being watched bursts through my bubble of solitude. I peek from behind the thick fringe of my eyelashes to scan around the pool. Slowly, my head turns to take in the entire area. Nothing. And it's silent, as though a predator lurks in the tree line.

The last things I want to confront are a jaguar or a bear. Hell, I'd even face a wolf before those two. I shudder and wade towards the grass as my eyes continue to search for any sign of a large animal. It's doubtful any of them are in this part of the park. But I'd rather be on land with a chance to run than floating in the water.

Once my feet touch the grass, I hurry towards my back-pack for the satellite phone. As I reach for the bag, a low growl reaches my ears. My head jerks in the sound's direction. I gasp at the sight of a giant red wolf with ice blue eyes. They flash silver as the wolf's gaze scans my body from head to toe. The rumbling in its chest washes over me.

My heartbeat quickens. Pupils dilate. Nipples pucker. Pussy quivers. My wobbly knees give out, and I land on my ass. But my eyes never leave the red wolf. Which, I swear, narrow then zoom to the apex of my thighs. I snap my legs together. He growls. I shiver, mouth slack on a moan.

I watch, captivated by his lethal power as he stalks towards me. Frozen in place, I whimper when his front paws land above my shoulders and his back legs part mine. His massive head lowers. I cry out, expecting him to rip my throat out. Instead, he nuzzles my neck as he rumbles deep in his chest. The vibrations roll through me, easing my soul. On a sigh, my eyes close as my head lolls to the side, exposing my vulnerable throat. His rumble morphs into a word.

"Mine."

Startled, my eyes pop open.

Bottomless ice blue eyes stare down at me. Fiery copper red hair trails down the face of the most gorgeous man I've ever seen. Chiseled cheekbones and strong jaw blend with long eyelashes and lush, full lips. Lips I can't stop myself from staring at with the hope they'll cover mine for a toe-curling passionate kiss.

"Mine."

I gasp at his possessive tone. He takes advantage of my open mouth and slants his over it. His tongue slips inside and tempts mine to join his in a tango. My gasp becomes a lusty moan. My back arches as my fingers grip his bulging biceps. Of their own accord, my legs wrap around his narrow hips and lock at the ankles. My heels dig into his firm ass to draw him to me. He lowers from a plank. The weight of his muscular body so much longer than mine presses me into the soft grass. My softness and curves mold to the hard planes of his body. I welcome him like an old lover even as my mind wonders what happened to the red wolf.

Balanced on his forearms, he reaches between us and fists his long, thick cock. With one brutal thrust, he plunges inside of my soaking wet pussy. I scream into his mouth as he stretches my inner walls with his girth. The bulbous tip bumps my womb. He grips the back of my neck and grinds his pelvis into mine. Locked in position beneath his hulking frame, I can only take what he gives me. With. Pleasure.

He rocks in and out of my spasming pussy with measured thrusts. My furled nipples brush against his firm pecs. The slight hair teases my sensitive flesh with each pass. He swallows my soft cries as they mix with his groans. Wave after wave of pleasure roll through my entire being as we move in sync like we've known one another for all time.

His controlled thrusts quicken to pistoning strokes as he makes demands of my body. He drops his head to suckle on my nipples, moving from one to the other until I writhe beneath him.

An orgasm starts in my toes and shoots up my thighs to detonate in my pussy. My back bows as my mouth jerks away from his. A scream rips from my throat. It reverberates around us. My body convulses from the intensity and continues to peak as he pummels into my pussy.

His feral growls join my screams to surround us with our mating cries. And it is a mating as he claims me for his own. His possession as clear as the sky above.

"Mine!"

His roar punches the air.

I shudder as another orgasm rips through me. It robs me of all ability to think and to speak. I can only feel. And he feels divine as he plunders my pussy. Then I cry out as he withdraws. He flips me onto my hands and knees before he plunges back inside my dripping core. I drop to my forearms with my face in the grass. I moan at his increasing thrusts.

The base of his cock swells. I yelp at the burn as he widens the entrance to my pussy. Instinctively, I wiggle away from the invasion. But he grabs my hips to still me. My fingers claw into the ground as he forces me to take his expanded cock. His groin slaps against my ass again and again. Breath escapes my lungs on the last thrust before a torrent of his seed jettisons into my womb.

Hot liquid drips on the back of my neck. A searing pain robs the last bit of air from my lungs. As I pass out, he growls.

"Mate!"

"Maya!"

"Maya, are you listening to your father and me?"

My mother Esmerelda Ariadna Garcia Diaz asks.

Her question rouses me from reliving the erotic dream from last night. It was the most vivid I've had over the last few weeks. They started as snippets during the night, with little more than the ghosting of another in my mind. The progression to a shadowed figure as though seen through a veil or a haze lasted longer. But last night... Oh. My. God.

My pussy clenches and moistens at the carnal memory. I shift on the seat of my Mercedes-Benz G-Wagen to ease the instant ache in my core for the mystery man. Yeah, to top it all off, I don't even know who he is. Aargh!

"You know, Maya, your father and I have been very lenient with you your entire life. Maybe too much. Do not allow our indulgence to influence you. You must come home now. It is your duty to our family…"

I bite back a moan—I mean a sigh, *focus, Maya*—as she drones on.

She and my father, Ricardo Armando Perez Gonzalez, call in their chit. They expect me to return to Caracas from Miami now that I'm twenty-five. The deal was to allow me to remain in the city after graduation from the University of Miami. Allow me the chance to live my life as I wished from eighteen until now.

I was thankful for the reprieve from my family. I love them to death. But I don't want to live under their rule. And a powerful rule it is since we're one of the wealthiest families in Venezuela and the world with the combination of my parents' families' petroleum companies through their arranged marriage.

And now it's my turn.

They want me to come home to marry a man I don't even know except by name—Emerico Tonio Santana Rodriguez. A man ten years older than me and a widower. Great, just great… Sure, he's only thirty-five and handsome. But still. He's not my choice. Don't I deserve to have my happily ever after like the women in my romance novels? I think so.

So, I delayed my return as much as possible.

My life in Miami is just as I want it. I've always been health conscious and met a woman at the gym who introduced me to fitness modeling. I successfully competed for three years, then became a personal trainer and wellness coach to help others on their fitness journey. And I'm damn good at it.

Even now, I wait in my truck for my client turned friend Wren Byrd. Our training session starts in five minutes. Unfortunately, my parents caught me before it started otherwise, my mobile would have been off, and I'd have missed their call. The call I've been dreading for months since my birthday.

Funny enough, the dream started right after I turned twenty-five.

Who the hell is this stranger who invades my dreams to tempt me with mind-blowing sex and the yearning for my soul mate? Why can't he appear and save me from my fate with Emerico? Dream lover, where are you???

A knock on my window jolts me.

Wren beams at me from outside the truck. My best friend just married the man of her dreams. Lucky girl.

Me?

"*Papá*, *Mamá*, I'm sorry. But my client just arrived. Can we continue our conversation later? I can call you tonight after my day ends."

They grouse but relent.

I'm not spoiled. But I am their baby girl—the youngest of their children with my brothers Odalis and Patricio three and two years older than me. All of them let me get away with more. However, I'm afraid the arranged marriage won't be one of the times.

With a sigh, I hop out of my truck and hug Wren.

"Hi, chica, don't you look all bubbly. You must be ready for your session, or Tag put it on you real good!"

She giggles as her face reddens and her mink brown eyes dance.

"Yes, and yes! Girl, I didn't know a male could be so voracious."

I grin and nod, thinking about the loser fiancé she had before she married Tag. What a difference a good man can make in a woman's life. Gee, I hope to know one day…

"Well, I'm more than happy for you, my friend. Now, let's get to it," I say as I grab my duffle bag from the back seat and loop arms with my bestie. "But don't think I'll go easy on you since you already had a workout for the day. No, ma'am!"

"I wouldn't expect anything less from you, drill sergeant!"

We giggle as we walk into the park next to Biscayne Bay. Other people exercise or play with their dogs on the open field of grass surrounded by palm trees blowing in the balmy breeze. The morning sun shines on us to start a new day in Miami. Just where I want to live my life as I wish.

Another sigh escapes. Wren pauses to glance up at me since I stand five inches taller than her at five feet, nine inches. Her eyes search my face for an explanation. However, I don't want to burden my newlywed bestie with my future husband drama.

"Let's start your warm-up with a jog to that spot over there. Ready, set, go!"

Wren yelps as I break free and charge ahead. Surprisingly, she catches up to me with ease. Not for the first time, I wonder how my BBW bestie is more fit since she married Tag. She was gaining strength and stamina with our thrice weekly training sessions. But her change in a few weeks is remarkable. I watch as she passes me then raises her arms in victory with a whoop.

The rest of the session goes just as smoothly, and I make a mental note to adjust her regimen.

"Tag and I are going to Club Hati with some other couples tonight. Come! I want you to meet everyone and hang out. It's been too long since we shook our booties, Maya."

I think about the impending phone call with my parents later and sigh.

"As much as I'd love to let loose, I have other plans," I respond, then continue when she pouts. "I know. I know. But I promise next time. Okay?"

"Fine. But I won't let you finagle your way out of it," Wren says, then hugs me before she heads for her car. She glances over her shoulder and waves.

I wave back with a forced smile. How I wish I could be so happily in love.

"Hey, there, Maya! I'm ready."

I pivot to find my next client. Drawing in a breath, I place a smile on my face and move on with my day.

Hours later, after the phone call with my parents and my promise to return home within the week, I decide to join Wren at Club Hati after all. I could use an escape from reality. I shower and change into a vintage crystal-embell-ished chain-mail mini dress and strappy sandals. My hair flows down my back with pink lip gloss and a bare face since I know I'm going to dance it up and don't want makeup dripping on my skin.

Which is why I take an Uber the short distance from my beachfront duplex penthouse to the club and not drive. I want to drink without concern for overindulging. And since Wren will be there with Tag, I have no worry about anyone getting out of hand with me.

I arrive at Club Hati and grin when I spot my friend in the DJ booth. I make my way to him since I can survey the club from the height of the raised booth to spy Wren. He greets me with a wink and points to the platform next to him. Happily, I walk to the steps where a bouncer helps me. I don't see my bestie, so I let the music take me away.

Eyes closed, I sway to the beat until the DJ taps me. I open my eyes, and he points to the stairs. My eyes widen. Wren stands next to the bouncer. My face splits in two as I wave her up. She turns and point at women with her. I nod and wave for them to come up, too.

The bouncer helps them navigate the steps in their high heels. Wren throws her arms around my neck for a hug before she introduces me to the others. My grin widens as I hug them, too. I motion for a moment and go to the DJ. I whisper in his ear to play Wren's anthem—T.I.'s "Live Your Life." He nods, and I return and wink at my bestie.

When the music blends to the song, she giggles and hugs me. We face the others and start dancing as Wren belts out Rihanna's lyrics. We dance from one song to the next.

A tingle at the back of my neck makes me pause and glance around.

Smoldering molten platinum eyes stare at me from the shadows.

Recognition dawns and a shiver courses through my body.

 *aya*

I CAN'T BELIEVE my eyes. It's the man from my dreams.

What type of psychedelic-ness is happening? How did he appear in my dreams and now stand in the shadows, watching me with an intense, heated stare? What the hell?

As the questions race through my mind, a nudge to my side interrupts their flow and any logical answers I can think of. I glance over to find Wren bumping her hip against my leg. She laughs and shimmies to the music.

I open my mouth to speak but need answers. My head swings back to the man. A niggling in the back of my mind tells me I know him from somewhere besides my dreams. And there's no doubt he's the man in each and every one of them, including the ones with his face obscured. My heart knows the truth. It races in my chest as I stare back at him, too entranced to dance.

"Hey! What's wrong?"

I blink as Wren talks over the music. She frowns and scans the dance floor. Her eyes widen when she notices the man. His eyes flash silver, and she gasps.

"What is it? Who is he?" I ask, frantic at her reaction to him as I glance between them. "Do you know who he is?"

Wren nods and places herself between the man and me.

"He's Viggo Larson, my Al—um… the younger brother of Jagger Larson and Tag's best friend. Do you know him?"

I shake my head and recall the names Wren mentioned over the last few months—Viggo amongst them. Relief washes over me. If she knows him, he can't be some weirdo. My gaze shifts to him.

His head tilts back as though he's sniffing the air.

Okay, maybe he is a bit odd.

"I could use a drink. Come back to the VIP section with me."

I flick my gaze to Wren, then back at Viggo. He's as handsome in person as he was in my dreams. Well over six feet, with an athletic build beneath his tailored suit. The contrast of his straightlaced appearance to the longer hair pulled in a knot with tattoos on the shaved sides of his scalp makes me wonder what kind of man he is. By the way women stare and nudge each other, they find him as attractive as I do. I bristle with jealousy when one approaches him.

He bends down and seems to sniff her, then shakes his head. His piercing eyes return to me. A jolt of electricity shoots through my body. I shake my head.

"Um, I'm going to dance a little longer. I'll come by after," I respond to Wren.

She eyes me, then glances over her shoulder.

"Are you sure?"

"Yes," I respond without hesitation.

She pauses before she nods and walks off, taking the other women with her.

I barely notice since my eyes remain riveted to Viggo Larson. The attraction between us is palpable. He continues to watch me despite another woman who stands before him, shaking her ass. I arch an eyebrow and turn my back. I'll give him a show he won't forget, and no woman can top.

My hands skim my hips and along my sides until my arms rise above my head. My hips move rhythmically as my ass wiggles to the beat. Only a moment passes before sizable hands grip my hips and a massive erection wedges between my butt cheeks. Warm breath blows across the delicate shell of my ear as a raspy voice growls.

"Mine!"

~

Viggo

. . .

HER!

The unique scent of fragrant frangipani mixed with fresh coconuts and salt carried on a tropical breeze from the Caribbean Sea fills my nostrils as I stalk closer to the beauty. All other females fall to the wayside. Their attempts to seduce me fail. My wolf recognizes his fated mate and wants no other. Neither do I.

When she turns her back to me and moves sensually, a howl threatens to leap from my mouth. I charge forward and grip her hips, pressing my front against her back to let her feel just how much I want to claim her.

Her scent engulfs me, triggering my senses. Serum leaks from my elongated fangs. My pheromones peak. My cock thickens and lengthens to the point of pain. I growl with need.

"Mine!"

She mewls as she leans against me. Her fingers pull at the hair tie, releasing my fiery mane. I groan as she tugs the long strands and trails her fingernails along my scalp. The bite of erotic pain heightens my obsession with her. She likes it rough. Perfect.

I growl low in my chest and undulate my hips, rocking her onto her toes. My cock pulses, eager to plunge into her pussy. The musky aroma of her arousal wafts up to my nose to blend with her unique scent. The thudding of her heart rings in my ears. My vision tunnels blocking all else around us.

We move as one to our own erotic beat.

My balls grow heavy as they fill with seed. Saliva and serum fill my mouth. The urge to claim her increases with each sway of our bodies.

Suddenly, she spins in my arms. Her gorgeous face tilts up. Topaz eyes gleam in the low light. The tip of her little pink tongue darts out to moisten her full lips. I watch, wondering how it will feel wrapped around my cock as I fuck her throat.

"I want you. Now."

My eyes jump to hers at the unexpected demand delivered in a husky, accented voice.

Without hesitation, I scoop her in my arms and stride down the stairs, across the dance floor, and up a flight from my office to my private suite. I added four suites exclusive to select members who want to continue their dancing between silk sheets. And I plan to do so and more with this beauty in my arms.

Inside my suite, I carry her to the bed and slide her down my body until she stands before me. Both hands cradle her face between them as I angle her head back to stare into the depths of her glittering eyes. They're still topaz. No hint of her inner wolf.

Fuck. Me.

She's a human female, not a she-wolf.

In my lust-filled haze and nostrils filled with her unique scent, I failed to notice she lacks the distinction of a wolf shifter. I lower my face to her neck and inhale deeply, hoping I'm mistaken. No. She's human.

My eyes squeeze shut on a frustrated groan.

The one thing I had no interest in enters my life.

The fear she'd be a human comes to pass.

I can't have her.

But my wolf refuses to back down. He pins me with a ferocious glare before he throws his head back. The piercing howl vibrates throughout my entire being. It shatters my resolve. He stares triumphantly.

Fine. I'll give in for one night. But I won't issue the claiming bite. I will not risk her life. Then we'll part ways. Better for me to face the possibility of madness from losing my fated mate than for her to die at my hands.

"Viggo?"

My eyes open as I startle, not expecting her to know my name. She smiles and places her hands on my chest to slide her fingers along the lapels.

"Rest easy, *amante*. I only ask for one night. Nothing more."

I lose myself in the depths of her topaz eyes. My hands clutch her face as my mouth crashes to hers. Only. One. Night. She gasps at the ferocity of my kiss. I take advantage of her open mouth to slide my tongue inside her wet warmth. It sweeps around to savor every bit as growls rumble in my throat. I will make the most of the night and the morning.

My tongue coaxes hers to meld with mine. Her sweet taste and soft cries drive me wild. I need more. So much more.

My hands slide down her body to grip the hem of her mini dress. With a flick of my wrists, it lifts and drops to the floor. I step back to admire her beauty. But she brings her hands up in an attempt to cover her bountiful tits. Oh, no. That will never do.

I lean forward and lift her hands away. Then my head lowers to lick her nipples. They're hard as pebbles and as delicious as ripe strawberries. The flat of my tongue laves one while my thumb and forefinger pinch and pull the other.

She mewls as her fingernails dig into my shoulders. Her back bows to present her tits to me for more attention. I oblige and suckle her plump nipples. Hard. She hisses but pulls me closer, eager for more.

My hands cup her round ass and squeeze each cheek. I lift her from her feet, and she wraps her arms around my neck. In one swift move, I toss her to the bed and watch as her tits bounce when she lands sprawled on her back. Wide eyes stare up at me in surprise. I growl and rip at my tie.

My clothes join hers in a pile on the floor. Naked, I stand by the bed staring down at her as my fist grips the base of my turgid cock. I squeeze then glide up, maintaining constant pressure over the thick, long, shaft. The plum-shaped tip drips with pre-cum. I smear it with the pad of my thumb over the head, biting back a groan. My wolf pants, tongue lolling, eyes bright, focused on the beauty.

No need for names.

Only. One. Night.

Braced on her elbows, hooded eyes follow my hand as it strokes my cock. Her lips part as the tip of her tongue slips out.

With a groan, I prowl from the foot of the bed and over her body until my knees bracket her shoulders, forcing her onto her back. My cock bobs in front of her face. Wide eyes stare at its enormity. Her jaw opens and closes. I smirk and fist the base of my cock then tap the tip against her lips. They part on a mewl.

"You will suck me. Every. Single. Inch."

Now, her mouth widens to accept my girth. I watch as my cock disappears inside. It brushes the soft palate, sliding deeper. Her eyes close as she struggles to take all my cock.

"Breathe through your nose. Relax your throat and let me in."

Her eyes pop open to lock with mine. So fucking gorgeous. I cup the back of her head as my cock moves beyond her gag reflex. She blinks and sputters. But I don't stop.

"Take me. All of me."

She nods.

"You're doing so well, beauty. You feel so good sucking my big cock in."

She blinks rapidly as my cock stretches her throat. The impression as it widens her neck makes my balls draw up, ready for release. She hums. The vibration travels along my cock straight to my heavy balls.

With a savage roar, I withdraw then snap my hips forward to plunge back in. She sputters as my movements increase in pace with thrusts and drags along her tongue and down her throat. When her lips kiss my groin, I let loose a torrent of jizz.

She struggles as her fingernails dig into my bulging thighs.

But I hold her firm commanding she breathe and consume every drop. When my hips slow to languid thrusts, releasing the last of my seed into her belly, I cup her face.

"Now, I will fuck your pussy, making you cum until you beg me to stop. Before we part, you will know I fucked you long and hard, ruining you for any other male. Do you understand?"

Her head bobs.

My still hard cock slips free. I swipe the tears from her eyes and lower my mouth to hers for a toe-curling kiss. She clings to me as I swallow her soft cries.

***

Maya

"ONE MORE, baby. Cum for me one more time..."

My well-used pussy spasms at Viggo's barked command. Juices leak past his giant dick buried deep inside my core. Even after hours of having sex, I still cannot believe my pussy stretches to accommodate his size. But the oh so delicious ache confirms it did each and every time. Just as it does now as the morning sun filters through the windows.

We barely slept.

He's like a feral beast who can't get enough. He's had me every which way possible—standing, against the wall, on all fours, planked above, kneeling. Incredible stamina.

I can barely keep up. He has me panting as though I ran the New York Marathon back-to-back three times. My arms ache and thighs burn. Talk about a never-ending workout session!

But this is just what I wanted. Only one night to do as I please before I return to Caracas and to the fate I never wanted. And I plan to leave Miami with a bang!

"Come on, baby…"

I draw on my reserves and tighten my pussy walls around his dick pounding inside of me. He growls as it throbs and grows larger. The orgasm starts in my toes, zings up my legs, and zaps my pussy. A hoarse scream tears from my sore throat—another hole he's plundered repeatedly. *Ay Dios mío.*

My entire body quakes from the earth-shattering impact. Boneless, I sag on his lap, thighs quivering around his hips.

He bands his arms around me, pressing me closer to his sweat-drenched chest where paw print tattoos mark his pecs. His hips jut up in the last throes of our fucking. He snarls as he cums. His body twitches as he buries his face in the crook of my wet neck.

I'm in a daze until hot cream coats my womb.

"Viggo! The condom! Did… Did it break?"

A feral growl sends shivers down my spine, even as my pussy clenches.

CHAPTER 4

 iggo

My wolf growls.

He wants to breed her. Issue the claiming bite to initiate her transformation to a she-wolf. Make her his forever.

For a moment, I hold her close as images flip through my mind's eye. Her belly round with my pup. She places my hand on a spot he kicked. Her gorgeous face glows as she smiles up at me. While we frolic in the Everglades with them in our wolf forms. My pup's excited yips as he chases a rabbit across the grass—

"Viggo!"

Fuck.

The images fade replaced by her face only this time it glows from post-coital bliss even if her eyes stare in shock.

I have the urge to cover her kiss-swollen lips with mine and drag her beneath me to pound her pussy—

"Viggo! You are not getting hard inside of me right now! *Ay Dios mío…* Let me go!"

Her palms press against my chest as she slides off my lap. She sucks in a breath and winces.

I feel bad for fucking her so hard. But I needed to get her out of my system since we'll never be together again. Unfortunately. I growl and shake my head. Enough! Now, focus.

"—don't believe in it. And then this happens."

I missed the first part of her sentence but don't miss her pointing to our combined juices dripping from her other swollen pussy lips. I bite back a growl as my cock thumps against my eight-pack abs. The head still slick leaks pre-cum through the remnants of the condom.

"Look what your monster dick did"—she gestures at the sheets as she crawls from the bed—"I have to take a shower. Hopefully, I can wash most of it away. I don't think I'm ovulating since I just had my period. Ugh!"

She stands staring at her inner thighs as my seed drips from her pussy. A frown mars her face when she glances up at me. It deepens when I sit entranced by the sight.

"Hey! Up here. You know what? Never mind," she says, then spins on her heel and marches to the en suite bathroom. Her ass jounces with each step. Damn.

I snap out of it when the door shuts behind her. My hand scrubs over my face as I consider the situation.

I've always worn a condom, and it never broke. I have

zero experience with this scenario. A she-wolf doesn't get pregnant outside of her heat. Since she's human, I guess the ovulation thing she mentioned prevents her from getting pregnant. We don't have a ton of information on the mating of male wolf shifters and human females for reference. Fuck if I know. I'll take her word for it.

My wolf whines, wanting to join her in the shower. I'm not so sure she'd welcome me. Or the boner I'm sporting. Besides, now's as good a time as any for the clean break. No pun intended.

I stride to the walk-in closet and throw on a pair of joggers. My cock tents the front, and I will it flaccid. Picking up my mobile, I wonder if she'd like breakfast. We ate before the kitchen closed for the night. But the number of calories burned makes me hungry as fuck. My metabolism is faster than a human. But I'm sure she's famished too.

Even though I want this to end now, I can't let her go without a decent meal. I'm a playboy, not a cad. Plus, she's Wren's friend. And I don't want Wren pissed at me for poor treatment of her.

Decision made, I place an order for delivery then plop on the bed. Nope. Don't want her to come out of the bathroom to find me lounging as though ready for another round. Instead, I sit at the café table by the window and check my messages.

A few minutes later, she emerges wrapped in my robe. She's tall but slight. The damn thing engulfs her with the belt around her waist twice. I hate to admit it, but she looks good in my clothes. I wouldn't mind her in the shirt she tosses on a chair as she searches for her mini dress. Her dress?

"Hey, I um… ordered breakfast. It'll be here in ten minutes. Afterwards, I can give you a ride home."

She shakes her head and tendrils of jet black hair slip from the topknot. They frame her face flushed rosy from the steam of the shower.

Again, I have the urge to cover both pairs of her swollen lips with my mouth and take her back to bed. My wolf and cock agree as both spring to stand tall.

"No. But thank you. I need to get home. It's not far. I'll get another Uber," she says as she unwinds the belt. I watch as she shrugs out of the robe and slips the dress over her head. It covers her glorious body from my hungry gaze.

My wolf whines. I groan.

She glances at me and cocks her head.

"You sure do make a lot of animalistic noises," she says, then adds. "Not that I mind."

The rosy glow on her cheeks deepen to crimson, and she ducks her head. She picks up her sandals and sits on the edge of the bed to slip them on her feet. She bends her knee, and I catch a glimpse and whiff of her pussy.

Fresh arousal greets my nostrils. I inhale deeply, hoping to imprint the tantalizing aroma along with the frangipani and coconuts on my mind. An indelible reminder of my fated mate, who will never be mine. My eyes close with a deep inhalation.

"Viggo?"

My eyes open as I exhale.

"I'm ready and the Uber will be here in three minutes. Will I be able to unlock the door to the club?"

I shake my head to clear it as I rise.

"No. I'll walk you out."

We walk through the empty club in silence. I demand my wolf back down as he paces and snarls. I don't need him to act up now. We're almost in the clear. A peek at her reveals a stoic expression on her face. Thankfully, she's not still upset about the condom.

I unlock the door and gesture her ahead of me. She pauses and glances at my face.

"Well, thank you for a lovely time, Viggo. Goodbye."

My heart constricts at the finality of her words. As the air rushes from my lungs, I cover the spot on my chest with a hand. I blink and nod, unable to speak.

She peers into my eyes for a second before she walks to the Uber.

I watch as the SUV pulls onto Ocean Drive. As it makes a U-turn, she raises her hand in farewell. Pain laces through me, and I lean against the doorframe. My head hangs as my wolf throws his back for a mournful howl.

～

Maya

. . .

"WHAT ARE the chances of me getting pregnant after a condom broke and I'm not ovulating?"

I hold my breath as I await an answer from Dr. Carmela Fuentes, my gynecologist. She knows I don't believe in birth control since they use synthetic hormones, and I put nothing in my body that's unnatural. Call me an extreme health nut all you want.

It's not like I've had many lovers. Viggo is only the second, and it's been over a year. So, no need for anything beyond a condom. Who knew his massive cock would break it? Aargh!

"Maya, it can still happen. You know my recommendation—"

"No. Okay, so I'll just have to wait and see. I truly doubt it, not that I'm an expert. Kindly email my medical records to my gynecologist in Caracas. Thank you, Dr. Fuentes."

I end the call and lean back against the chaise lounge on my terrace. The Atlantic Ocean spreads out before me. Its turquoise water sparkles like diamonds in the morning light. Jet skiers zip by and megayachts cruise along while a parasail carries a couple above its surface. I inhale and relax on the exhale.

Only a few days remain before I leave Miami. I refuse to spend my precious time worrying about anything, including the potential of a pregnancy. I have other things to focus on. Over the next few hours, I call my clients, cancel other appointments, and organize my move with Idania—my mother's personal assistant.

By the time I finish, I need to go for a run to clear my

head. After I change into a crop top with matching shorts and sneakers, I pull my hair into a ponytail and attach my mobile to the armband. Popping earbuds in, I head for the beach.

The balmy breeze from the Atlantic Ocean does little to ease the warm rays of the sun. But I don't mind. I love the Miami weather. Hell, I love everything about my adopted city. I let my mind wander as I run along Ocean Drive. Then Club Hati comes into view.

My eyes lift to the windows where I guess Viggo's suite is based on the times he fucked me against the wall of glass. I bite my lower lip as a moan erupts from my throat. Despite the heat, my nipples pucker beneath my sports bra. I dash by the club. Better to put it all behind me.

However, my mind disagrees. It replays the hours we shared. Sure, we had lots of sex. But a few intimate moments took place between us. When food arrived from the kitchen, he sat me on his lap at the café table and hand fed me bits of steak. I balked. But he had none of it. I moan as I recall how he swatted my butt when I wrapped my tongue around the asparagus spear like it was his dick. Later, he recreated the scene, much to my delight. His cock is as beautiful and tasty as it is large.

He's a work of art—all sculpted lean muscle, long legs, sizable hands, handsome face, captivating ice blue eyes. Man, oh man, is Viggo Larson H-O-T.

Too bad we don't have a chance.

The thought is like ice water dumped over my heated body. I gasp and stop, placing my hands on my knees to catch my breath. I didn't think he'd have such an impact on me and would be the perfect one-night stand for a last hurrah. But I can't stop thinking about him even while focused on my calls or while running. He's gotten under my skin.

Call from Wren Byrd.

In my ear, the disembodied voice of my mobile announces the call from my bestie. How apropos.

"Hey, chica!"

"Hey, nothing, missy. What happened last night?"

Good grief. My bestie's radar is on full alert. Since I hadn't heard from her after she gave me the side-eye last night, I figured she'd forgotten about the heated exchange between Viggo and me. Guessed wrong. Plus, I have to tell her the day has come for me to return to Caracas.

"We need more than a phone call for this convo. It requires a face-to-face. How about I come to your new place with Tag?"

Wren pauses.

I've noticed she's always hesitant for me to come to Moon Island, where Tag has a beachfront mansion. It's a super exclusive private island in Biscayne Bay, across from South Beach. I've only gotten glimpses of it as I drive by the wrought-iron gates with a security booth off the MacArthur Causeway. I'd love a chance to see it before I leave. But her response nixes it as usual. I'll have to ask her why the secrecy.

"How about I come by your place in an hour? I'll bring some of your favorite snacks. We'll drink mojitos while you tell me everything. And I mean every single detail. Good?"

"Fine, Secret Squirrel. But in exchange, you'll have to tell me why you block me from Moon Island."

She's silent a moment, then responds, "See you soon, chica!"

I shake my head as I end the call and check the time. An hour gives me time to finish my run and shower before Wren arrives. I cast a last glance at the third-floor windows of Club Hati. With a sigh, I jog away.

An hour later, Wren and I sit on my terrace. A frosty mojito pitcher and a tasty variety of finger foods— including my favorite Cuban beef patties and grilled shrimp kabobs—sit on the table between us. The second I finish my first bite of an empanada, she pounces.

"So, what happened?"

I stall for time with a sip of my drink. She's my bestie, so I have no problem sharing. Well, aside from the exact details of Viggo using the flat of his tongue to make me cum so hard I saw stars before I blacked out...

"First, I have some bad news."

She gasps as wide eyes scan my neck.

"Viggo didn't bi—I mean hurt you, did he? I wasn't going to say anything. But his scent is all over you!"

I blink, confused.

"What do you mean? I showered twice since I left him. How do you smell him on me?" I ask as I lift my t-shirt for a sniff. "I only smell my citrus bodywash. Are you sure?"

Her cheeks flush scarlet as she shakes her head. Her

mahogany hair forms a curtain, blocking her face from my questioning stare. She mumbles a response then speaks louder when I huff.

"I don't know. Maybe his cologne lingers in your hair or something? Never mind that. Tell me the bad news. You're scaring me."

"My parents called yesterday to demand I return to Caracas for the arranged marriage. I leave in a few days. It's terrible!"

"No! You can't go! I thought they changed their minds since your birthday passed months ago. Can't we do something to dissuade them? Look what happened with Jonathan and me until Tag came along. Don't let them force you to marry someone you don't love, let alone even know. It's unfair and cruel!"

Tears well in my eyes as my best friend offers suggestions to change their minds. But I've always known I'd have an arranged marriage. It's just the way it works in our circle, no different from Wren's. She was lucky to meet Tag before she made the mistake of marrying that *tramposo* Jonathan and went against her uncle's arrangement. I see nothing that can help me. I'm pretty resigned.

"It's okay, Wren. But you have to promise to visit me. And I'll fly up a few times a year. We can still be besties, even long distance," I say with a forced smile. No point in ruining our last few days together. "Now, let me tell you about that hottie, Viggo Larson. He reminds me of those sexy Vikings from the TV shows. Boy, oh, boy!"

Her frown changes into a smile as she giggles at me,

fanning my face. She listens intently as I give her the deets. Her eyes widen when I tell her about the animalistic noises he made and how his eyes flashed silver. From time to time, her gaze flicks to my neck. When I ask why, she waves her hands and tells me to continue. I shrug and finish with the broken condom.

"What?!?!?! You're not on birth control, and I doubt you'll take emergency contraceptives."

"Don't worry. I just finished my period. No ovulation, no pregnancy. I'm glad my last Miami hurrah was with Viggo. Too bad we hadn't hooked up when you first met Tag. If I'd known Viggo is his best friend, we would have gone on double dates! But I'm grateful and a firm believer in things happen when they should. Now, let's get drunk!"

CHAPTER 5

iggo

THANK YOU, Miami, for being such an amazing part of my life for the past eight years! I'll miss you! Adiós!

My heart skips a beat.

Maya's gorgeous face stares at me from my tablet.

As has become my habit over the last few days, I stalk her social media posts. My mind wouldn't stop thinking about her. So, I checked Wren's feed, found the link to her best friend, and learned her name.

Maya Alejandra Perez Garcia.

I devoured each post, wanting to learn all I could about the beauty. A former fitness model turned personal trainer. No wonder she has such a banging body. My wolf growls at images of her with male clients, especially when she touches them.

However, seeing her soothes my wolf and gives me a reprieve from his constant whining and snarling. Sure, I want to howl too. But I believe it's best we stay apart. The risk to Maya is too great even if I ache to be with her. So far, losing myself in her social media staves off any sign of madness.

But this latest video nearly undoes me.

I only caught the end of her live stream, so it stops in moments. The only clues I have to her whereabouts is the area around her as she spins, holding the camera up for a selfie. She's on the beach, close to Club Hati.

I don't need my wolf's urging to race from my beach-front penthouse further up Ocean Drive. Once I hit the street, my pace slows to avoid stares at my superhuman speed. As the breeze enters my nose, I scent the air to pinpoint her location.

Unfortunately, it's a busy Saturday with throngs of tourists and locals. They stroll along on the sidewalks and blanket the beach. I zip around them until I get to the spot I guess she stood. Only a trace of coconuts and frangipani lingers amongst the other scents.

My eyes dart about, frantic to find Maya. I don't spot a female in a white tank top and leggings amongst the myriad of other beachgoers or on the sidewalk. It didn't take me but ten minutes. But it's enough time for her to disappear.

With a frustrated growl, I storm back to my condo. All

is a blur until I reach the garage and bump into a male wolf shifter.

The Miami Pack owns the forty-story building for unmated males to live if they don't live on Moon Island with the rest of the pack. It's our principal residence where Jagger, Tag, Dylan, and my parents with Signy have mansions. Not too long ago, Rust lived on the top floor since he's older than me. My penthouse takes up the one below his former pad.

The male takes one look at me and throws his hands up as he bares his neck in submission. I grumble an apology and stalk to my Ducati. The motorcycle engine revs and the back wheel screeches as I drive out of the garage.

I head to Moon Island, where I expect to get answers from Wren. She'll know what the hell Maya's talking about. I zig and zag my way along Collins Avenue to the cause-way. Minutes later, I turn off the causeway and pull up to the intricate wrought-iron gates—the entrance to Moon Island. Two members of the security team sit in a guard-house. They recognize me and wave as the gates open. I nod and rev the engine, eager to pass through.

I make a beeline for Tag's home, ignoring the posh resi-dences ranging from ranch style to two- and three-story along the main road. I pull into the driveway of his grand Mediterranean Revival style mansion on Biscayne Bay. Turning off the engine, I hop off the bike and jog to the glass and metalwork double doors. The doorbell chimes, and I pace, waiting for Tag to open them.

"Where's Wren?"

"The fuck you mean, 'where's Wren?' What do you want with my mate?"

He snarls as his emerald green eyes flash with his wolf just below the surface. An inch taller than me and bulkier, he puffs up his chest possessively.

I'm already on edge and curl my lip, baring my fangs.

"Hold on there, boys! Play nice."

Wren steps between us with her arms outstretched. She flicks her gaze from one to the other. My expression gives her pause.

"Did something happen with Maya?"

Tag frowns and sniffs the air. Then a sly grin spreads across his face as his eyes gleam with mirth.

"Let me guess… You finally met your match, playboy!"

He guffaws while I growl.

"To answer you, Wren, nothing happened aside from the other night. But I need to know what she's talking about in her live video."

Wren nods and gestures for me to follow her into the house. Tag brings up the rear, still chuckling. Fucker.

"Let me see what Maya posted first," she says as she sits on the sofa and picks up her mobile. She nods as she listens to the entire post.

My heart clenches anew.

Maya left for the airport.

"Where is she going? I—I want to say goodbye."

Wren shakes her head as she stares at me. Pity fills her eyes.

"Why not?" I demand, wolf bristling.

"Easy, bro. Watch your tone with Wren."

"It's okay, Tag," she says, then turns to face me. "What is Maya to you, a one-night stand or something more?"

I shrug, trying to make light of it before I respond.

"I'm not sure. We had a good time. It's just weird she didn't mention leaving. Where is she going?"

Wren studies my face. I put on what I hope translates to a nonchalant expression even while my wolf rages inside. Wren sighs.

"Well then, it shouldn't matter to you, and you came all this way for nothing, Viggo," she says with an arched eyebrow. Her challenging expression lets me know she sees right through my facade.

"Fine. She may be my fated mate. At least her unique scent and my wolf's reaction make me wonder."

Wren gasps and covers her mouth with her hand.

"Oh, no! I mean, that's good. But…"

She trails off, and I jump to my feet.

"But what, Wren? Tell me!"

Tag growls and leaps to his feet. He pushes me back onto the chair and hovers over me with fangs extended and eyes feral. I glare back with a snarl.

"I want answers! No more hemming and hawing."

"Okay, okay. You're right, Viggo. If Maya may be your fated mate, you deserve to know the truth. Tag, baby, please sit. You'd act the same way if you needed information about me."

Tag narrows his eyes at me, but his wolf returns to the

depths of his being. He pivots and sits beside Wren, taking her hand in his.

She kisses his cheek, and he smiles down at her. Their obvious love makes me ache for Maya even more. I close my eyes as my hand rubs my chest.

"Viggo, don't go berserk."

My eyes pop open as alarms ring in my head. This will not be good. I can sense it but nod, wanting answers.

"Maya is from an extremely wealthy family that arranged for her to marry a—"

A bestial roar splits the air. It reverberates around the living room.

My vision reddens as my wolf surges to the forefront. The sensations of my bones reshaping and muscles lengthening to shift me from my human form to that of my great red wolf block out all else. Crackling and a flash find me on all four massive paws within moments. Ignoring Tag and Wren's cries to stop, my beast runs for the open sliding glass doors. He bounds onto the deck, over the side, and lands on the grass before racing to the center of the island.

Another perk of our private island provides is a safe place for members of the pack to run in wolf form unencumbered. We run as a full pack in the Everglades a few times a month. The vast expanse and relative safety the subtropical wilderness offers makes an ideal setting for our numbers.

However, now, the island's oasis calls to me. I need to outrun the pain in my chest and the frustration in my mind. My fated mate is bound for another. Flying to another male's arms. A forlorn howl pours from my throat.

I run past fragrant gardenia and jasmine bushes. Their floral scents fill my nose. But don't mask the unique scent of Maya. I can never forget it. With a snort, I dash between some palm trees.

Glimpses of other pack members in wolf form appear amongst the foliage. Not wanting to interact, I increase my speed and head towards the other end of Moon Island. I run for what seems hours. A normal wolf would have tired by then, muscles strained to capacity. As a wolf shifter, my body heals quickly unless silver is involved. Then it can be fatal.

I drag my weary body back to Tag and Wren's deck. My best friend rises from a chair and holds a t-shirt and a pair of joggers in his hand. Gone is the possessive anger in his face, replaced by concern. Unfortunately, the pain in my heart doesn't abate as I shift and put on the clothes. Not that I mind being in the buff. Another distinction between shifters of any kind and humans, nudity is natural. But Tag doesn't want my ass out with Wren nearby.

I run my fingers through my wild hair and drop onto the chair next to his. He hands a tumbler filled with amber liquid to me. I toss it back in one gulp then refill it from the decanter on the table. Downing that one, I pour another and lean forward with my elbows on my thighs and my head hanging. I twirl the tumbler and watch the sunset as prisms in the crystal.

Tag sips his Scotch in silence, giving me the time I need.

"Here's to not wanting a fated mate to having one for a night then losing her to another," I say as I raise my glass in a mock toast. "But you know what? It's for the best. She's a human, and I will not risk her life with the transformation into a she-wolf."

Tag cocks his head and pins me with an intense stare.

"You do realize Wren was a human female before I claimed her, right? So, why can't you do the same with Maya?"

"It would kill me if something happened to her. You know that woman the male wolf shifter turned all those years ago died?"

"And the wolf madness that overtook him? What about that?"

"Well, I'll just have to wait and see."

Maya

"WE'LL LAND in just over three hours, *Señorita* Maya. Would you care for a beverage before we take off?"

"No, thank you. Once we're airborne, I'll have some water and a light meal."

The flight attendant bows his head and returns to the crew compartment.

My parents sent one of their private jets to deliver me back to Caracas. I left Idania to finish up the loose ends in

Miami. She'll return on a commercial flight in a few days even though I offered to wait. But my parents insisted I return immediately. They probably think I'll run away. I wish I could.

With a sigh, I stare out the window as the jet taxis to an airstrip of Miami International Airport. I can't believe I'll be in Venezuela in a short while. I'd hoped this day would never come. However, I knew it would. What I didn't expect was to miss not only the city I've called my second home but the man who I can't stop thinking about. The one-nighter I thought would end in hours still dominates my thoughts days later.

I haven't heard from him. I'd figured he may try to reach me through Wren. But he didn't. No word. Not a peep. He didn't even show up to my going away party Wren threw for me at Sol Beach Club last night. So, I guess I was just another night's fuck for him. Well, it's what I wanted. But why does my heart ache and my head swivel to watch Miami drop away through gray clouds?

Once it's obscured by the stormy fluff, I lean back in the plush leather chair. My eyes close as tears flow down my cheeks like raindrops from the clouds in the surrounding sky.

 *aya*

"I KNOW this is your engagement party. But I still don't understand why you don't want to wear the white gown I picked for you. This dress is lovely on you. Why wouldn't you want to wear white, Maya?"

My mother frets about me as I stand in the living room of my parents' penthouse in the Los Palos Grandes neighborhood. It has a view of Waraira Repano National Park. Seeing it reminds me of the dream I had with Viggo shifting from a wolf into a man.

Weirdly, my dreams of him have only increased over these past two weeks since I left Miami. Many nights I awake from the intensity of an orgasm as I cry out his name. The sheets tangle around my sweat-drenched body as they cling to me while my heart beats against my ribs. My eyes open to the empty bedroom of my apartment and not to Viggo's handsome face above me. My heart and body ache for my Viking lover.

Even now, a flush creeps from my breast to my cheeks.

I shake my head to clear it before I face my mother. The gold lamé gown swirls around my ankles. The draped origami folds turn back to reveal the length of my legs while the strapless top and open back show off my toned arms and back. Black stilettos and clutch complete my look.

Why should I wear white when the gold complements my skin better? Who cares about it being for my engagement party? I'll wear what I please to have some control over the night.

"*Mamá*, I prefer this dress. But thank you for your thoughtfulness."

"You do, *cariño*. Emerico will be proud," my father says as he and my brothers stride into the living room. "He's on his way up now."

I avert my gaze as he kisses my cheek. For a moment, my heart constricts and my breathing falters. I fear a panic attack will drop me to the floor. A gasp escapes my parted lips, and I cling to my father's forearms to steady myself on legs that threaten to give out.

"Are you all right?"

In response to Patricio's question, I nod my head, not trusting my voice. I sense his gaze as he studies my face.

We're closer than I am to Odalis. So, I know better than to return Patricio's stare. He'll see right through me.

"*Señor* Emerico Tonio Santana Rodriguez."

My stomach flips as the butler announces my intended fiancé's arrival. A business trip kept him away until now. I press a hand over my belly to will away the distress. I suck in a breath then give myself a silent pep talk and send a prayer for strength to get through this farce of a marriage.

"Emerico! Here's your blushing bride!"

My father grins wider than the Cheshire Cat as he holds my elbow and turns to face Emerico. His brown eyes assess me from head to toe. Under his scrutiny, my back straightens, and I lift my chin. *You can do this, Maya!*

"A pleasure to meet you at last, Maya. How stunning you are."

He extends his hands as he approaches me. I guess he's six feet tall since I have an inch on him in my stilettos. When his lips press to my cheeks, I fight the urge to recoil. His warm breath laced with cinnamon makes my stomach churn. I bite back a gag and paste a smile on my face.

"The pleasure is mine, Emerico," I manage, without a hitch in my voice.

He turns to my parents and brothers to shake their hands and to kiss my mother's cheeks. I watch as she fawns over him, and the men grin. My stomach roils again.

"Maya, may I have a word with you on the terrace?"

I swallow back bile knowing he's going to propose so I'll have the engagement ring on before we leave for the party. Hundreds of guests gather in the hotel's ballroom, eager to congratulate us. The official press release goes out in the morning. Soon photos of the happy couple will splash across websites, newspapers, and magazines. *Vogue* plans a cover feature to follow me from the engagement party through the wedding day. Designers vie to dress me. I couldn't care less.

Drawing on my strength, I nod and place my hand on his offered forearm. I catch my mother smiling up at my father with tears in her eyes. Great…

Emerico closes the glass sliding door behind us and leads me to the table, where he helps me into a chair. I smile my thanks and adjust my gown. His gaze drops to my legs and travels up to the top of the slit. I cringe and cross my legs, placing my hands on the dress to keep it closed. He frowns and settles in the chair next to me.

"Maya, we may not know one another. But I want to assure you I will treat you with the utmost respect, care for you, and support you in the means you're accustomed to as a woman of your standing. In return, I require your respect, faithfulness, and for you to bear my heirs. You will want for nothing. Do you understand?"

I swallow back a retort and agree. No use in prolonging the inevitable. And on cue, he removes a navy blue velvet box from his tuxedo jacket pocket. Tears well in my eyes, not from joy. Rather from a profound sadness that sucks the air from my lungs. Once again, I press a hand to my belly and breathe deeply to invoke calm in my body.

"Don't cry, *bella*," he says, mistaking the tears leaking

from my eyes for happiness. He hands a handkerchief to me and waits while I dab my eyes.

I want to throw myself on the floor and bawl. But I suck it up. *Get it over with, Maya.*

He reaches for my left hand and slides the pear cut diamond ring on my finger. It's loose, but he smiles.

"We'll get it sized tomorrow. Tonight, I want all to see you belong to me, Maya Alejandra Perez Garcia."

He leans over and presses his mouth to mine.

I can't open it for fear I'll vomit. So, I make a smacking noise and lean back in the chair, using the excuse of wiping tears from my eyes. He grins and stands.

"Come, *bella*, let us celebrate our union," he says as he extends his arm.

I can only nod as I loop my arm through his.

My family cheers when we re-enter the living room. My mother oohs and aahs over the ring. It's gorgeous, but from the wrong man. I can only think of Viggo and what it would be like to marry him. An arm around my waist draws me from my musings. I glance up to find my second oldest brother.

Patricio pulls me aside.

"Is this what you truly want, Maya?"

Topaz eyes so like mine stare down at me as he searches my face for the answer. It's no use in going back now. So, I force a smile on my face and nod.

"All will be well, brother of mine. Thank you."

He studies me for a moment longer. Then Emerico calls

to me. I smile once more at my brother and move to my fiancé's side.

"This is the start of a beautiful partnership between our families. Let us enjoy this night and many more to come!"

My head bows as I swallow a sob while the others cheer.

It is done.

~

Viggo

"Oh, Viggo! Yes. Yes. Yes!"

I pound into Maya as she writhes beneath me, screaming my name. Her forehead rests on the silk sheets with her delectable ass up high gripped between my hands. I stare as my cock thrusts in and out of her hot, slick pussy, stretching it to a gaping hole I want to explore.

Her pussy walls clamp onto my cock like a vise, eliciting a feral growl from the depths of my soul.

"Who's pussy is this?! Who do you belong to?!"

I snarl as each thrust drives her deeper into the mattress.

She keens with another toe-curling orgasm. Her pussy milks my cock, demanding me to fill her womb with my seed.

Not yet.

"I will not cum until you give me three more orgasms. Starting. Right. Now!"

I emphasize each word with a forceful thrust. My balls slap her ass as my tip strikes her G-spot.

She screams for no more, even as she rocks her ass back against my groin.

"You're a contradiction, little girl. Do you want this or not?!"

"*Ay Dios mío! Sí! Sí! Sí!*"

Her wail as she cums hard stiffens my cock. But I refuse to give her my knot to prepare for my seed to fill her womb and make her belly round with my pup.

"Two. More!"

She pants and claws at the sheets. The silk rips as she tosses her head side to side. Desperate moans pour from her slack mouth.

"Viggo! Please!"

One hand slides around her hip to cup her bare mons. Two fingers delve inside while my thumb circles her clit. When I pinch the sensitive bud, she clenches her pussy walls as her back bows.

"There's my good girl. One. More! Do you want my seed to coat your womb or not?!"

Her head bobs as she pants. Then she yelps when my palm connects with her ass for a resounding spank.

"Words, little girl! I will have your words!"

"*Sí!*"

I growl barbarically as she strangles my engorged cock. My balls fill with seed as the tingle lurking at the base of my spine becomes an electric bolt of lightning. It wends its way to my balls, along my cock initiating my knot, and zaps the tip to release a copious amount of my seed deep within her womb.

"Only. Mine. Forever!"

I bark in her ear as my knot locks her to me. Hot, creamy seed bursts forth to create my pup inside my fated mate. My hips continue to piston as her pussy milks my cock for every single drop. When I have no more to give, I collapse on top of her, pushing her to spread out on the bed.

The weight of my body covers her as my face buries in her neck. My fangs extend with serum dripping from them. I push her sweat-dampened hair aside and clamp down on the juncture of her neck and shoulder, issuing my claiming bite. She will bear my scent and transform into a she-wolf. Mine for all time.

Still locked together by my knot, I roll us to our sides and envelop her with my body. One hand cups a tit and the other her mons. With my face buried in her hair, I let sleep take me.

The ringing of my mobile awakes me from yet another dream about Maya. I groan when I realize it's a wet dream as jizz pools on the body pillow I'm wrapped around and on the tangled sheets. Great. Now, I've reverted to a randy teenage male. I scrub a hand over my face as I turn off the alarm on my mobile.

I cast a longing glance at the silver-framed photos of her on the nightstand. In one shot, she's on the beach in a white bikini. She's radiant as the sun shines on her glistening golden skin and her topaz eyes sparkle. She's laughing at the person holding the camera. My wolf growls as I wonder for the hundredth time if a male captured her beauty.

I turn to the pillow beside mine, where I placed a copy of the selfie she took one morning when she awoke in her bed. I never understood why people posted such images on their social media for all the world to see a private moment. But I'm damned glad Maya posted one. Her tousled jet black hair fans around her head as sleepy eyes stare up at the camera. Her full lips curve into a secret smile. Again, my wolf growls. Who the hell put that sated look on her face?

Two weeks of nightly dreams starring Maya and surrounding myself with her images do nothing to ease the constant ache in my chest. I drop back onto the pillows and unlock my mobile. A photo of Maya in a flexy-bendy yoga pose greets me as my wallpaper. I study the lines of her body in the white unitard. Long, toned, curves in all the right places. I groan as my cock thickens and lengthens. I give it a few strokes to ease the ache before I check the Google alerts I set to track her name over the Internet. If any news bears her name, I'll know all about it in moments.

Stalker much? Hell, yeah. She's my obsession. And I don't give a damn.

If I can't have her, I will know what she's up to.

Wren gave me the rest of the story about the arranged

marriage and return to Caracas. I had my guy run an extensive background check on the fucker she's engaged to. No red flags. But I monitor him too. If he hurts her, I'll rip his throat out with my fangs and eat his heart straight from his chest. I can't have Maya. But I'll be damned if I let anyone hurt her.

No recent news on the alerts.

I close my eyes a moment and let my mind replay the latest dream. If only she were here beside me, sated and cuddled in my arms. My wolf whines. He's inconsolable. But I ignore him for the greater good. No harm to Maya.

After a while, I roll out of bed and stride to the en suite for a shower. Time to face a new day. Without my fated mate.

"Brother, you look like shit."

"Yeah, Viggo. Not getting much sleep?"

I roll my eyes at Jagger and Tag as I lower into a seat at the table on the executive floor of Larson Enterprises. It's time for the weekly division update meeting. We're the first ones in the conference room. Now, I wish I wasn't trying so hard to be taken seriously and arrived last. Anything to avoid my older brother and best friend's stares.

"Tag told me about Maya. My question is why didn't you come to me first?"

I shrug and spin my pen on the table's sleek surface. Tag wouldn't have known if I didn't have to ask Wren for answers. With my brother and our best friends mated, I prefer not to go into the details of my current abysmal love life. Best to stick with the stalking than to have in-depth discussions and Jagger putting the kibosh on it.

"Not an answer, Viggo. I'm asking as your older brother, not as your Alpha. Talk to me. I'll help."

I glance over at him as I consider his offer. He knows what it's like to lose his fated mate, even if he didn't remember until years later. I check my watch. We have ten minutes before the others arrive. I spill the whole sorry tale.

"Damn. That's a tough one. But you realize she may survive the claiming bite and transition. Isn't it better to try than to lose her forever?"

"I told him the same thing," Tag adds. "Look at Wren. She's adjusted just fine. But I understand your concern. Hell, I nearly lost my mind waiting for her to awaken from the transition."

I pause to consider since it's getting harder to be apart from Maya knowing she's with another male who plans to marry her. Then I shake my head.

"She doesn't know what she is to me, and it's better to keep it that way. Let her live her life. Better only I suffer than something happens to her—"

"Or she rejects you."

My eyes widen at Jagger's comment. Could that be it too? There's a chance she won't accept me as a wolf shifter. Freak out at the enormity of the situation. Then I'd have to ask Sage to wipe Maya's mind so she can't tell other humans about us. That would be a major catastrophe for not only wolf shifters but other paranormals. Humans would hunt us down for science and drive us into extinction.

I shudder at the thought.

"Maybe. But I won't have to worry about that now, will I?"

Jagger doesn't have time to answer since the doors open and the heads of divisions walk in. He and Tag eye me for a moment before he starts the meeting.

I sigh in relief.

I dodged a bullet… A silver bullet.

CHAPTER 7

 *iggo*

"You know you should have spoken to me about Maya. I'm a female and can give you my perspective better than your boys. What do they know about how a female feels? They can only comment on secondhand info and what they think is the case. Now, tell me everything from the beginning. Correction, not the sex part. Leave all of that out, thank you very much. Eeew!"

As bad as I feel, I can't help but to chuckle at my younger sister's expression as she puts a hand over her mouth and gags. The sun glints off her oversized shades as she shakes her head and wrinkles her nose.

We're at Sol Beach Club on South Beach—another of Larson Enterprises' properties under my purview. It's across the street from Club Sol & Mani South Beach, the flagship of six exclusive, luxury, members only BDSM clubs for wolf shifters. The beach club is an extension of it but also caters to humans and other paranormals.

It's Saturday, so Signy insisted I *quit moping at home and hang out* with her for the day. She showed up at my penthouse and waited while I got ready. Now, we sit cross-legged on the raised sunbed in our cabana. The white canvas curtains remain tied to the four posts for an unobstructed view of the azure waters of the Atlantic Ocean as it stretches to the horizon. A teak table with eight white canvas and teak chairs stands at the foot of the sunbed, where we'll eat lunch later.

It's a busy morning with the other cabanas, low sunbeds, and chaise lounges occupied. Most people opt to keep the umbrellas closed to take advantage of the warm sun. Their colorful bikinis and board shorts add to the tropical atmosphere. Sun glistens on oiled skin or dries the droplets from a dip in the water. Still others sit at the restaurant and bar for brunch.

Sol Beach Cub South Beach proves another of my successes for our family's company.

I take a deep breath and inhale the saltwater breeze. It bears no resemblance to Maya's unique scent. But it still reminds me of her. With a sigh, I face Signy and tell her what happened, leaving out the sex and, of course, the stalking.

"Oh, Viggo. You should give Maya the chance to decide

what she wants to do. You can't make such a decision one-sided. It impacts both of your lives."

I run a hand through the length of my hair, loose from the bun. A tug to the ends pricks my scalp and clears my head.

Everyone keeps telling me the same thing. Was I wrong in letting Maya go without revealing what I am, who we are to one another, and letting her decide the course she wants her life to take? Is it too late? What the hell should I do now?

As though sensing my thoughts, Signy places a hand on my arm. She takes her sunglasses off to stare into my eyes. Like Jagger and me, she has the Larson trait of ice blue eyes. Hers show concern as she speaks.

"Viggo, it's never too late to go after the one you love. And Maya is your fated mate. You know it's true, so stop trying to deny it. She's not married yet and deserves the right to know what fate plans for her."

She squeezes my arm and smiles.

"You can thank me later. Now, let's go for a swim. Last one in is a rotten egg!"

She leaps from the sunbed with the grace of a she-wolf and races for the water. Sand flies with each step. Males turn to stare as she zips by in a white bikini, all long legs with waist-length black hair flying behind her, and giggles in her wake.

I glare at them as I chase after her. They flinch at the ferocity. The wolf shifters don't dare to challenge me. Humans lower their eyes. No fucker is good enough for my baby sister! The males who come to court her will face Jagger and me first, not to mention Tag, Dylan, and Rust. Good luck, suckers.

I catch Signy up by the waist and wade into the water. She squeals and flails her arms when I throw her into a wave. She reemerges spluttering as she wipes her eyes. I chuckle and dive in. She jumps on me and pushes me further beneath the surface. We tussle like we did as kids when she was more tomboy than glamour girl. It's fun to let loose with my little sister.

We go for a swim then float on our backs, staring up at the cloudless blue sky. My ears pick up the chatter of human females around us.

"He's so tall."

"Damn, he's sexy AF!"

"I wonder if they're a couple."

"Get a look at what he's packing in those board shorts. Oh!"

I close my eyes and roll over to swim away from them. Not too long ago, I'd have flirted with the females and fucked them all if they were game. Now, no interest whatsoever. Only one woman will do for me. And I'm still not convinced I can have her.

"Hey, let's get some Jet Skis. I'll race you," I say to Signy as I swim up to her.

She grins, and we swim to the water sports section. A male who's a pack bachelor recognizes us and rushes to help. His eyes zoom in on Signy. I growl low in my chest. He bows his head in deference to the pack prince and princess. Signy rolls her eyes at me and sashays to the life vests as she giggles. We gear up and hop onto the Jet Skis.

We zip along the shore, going north to Mid-Beach, then south past South Beach to Fisher Island and back. Signy makes figure eights, and I skim over their wakes. We spot a few sea turtles and a pod of dolphins. Boaters wave as we go by. Once we return to the beach, we decide it's time for lunch.

After quick showers to rinse off the saltwater, we sit at the table in front of our cabana. A server comes by and takes our orders of grilled seafood and French fries. We laugh and talk while we sip mojitos.

"Now, the party can get started!"

"Make way!"

We glance up to find our brother, Sage, Tag, Wren, Rust, Natalie, Dylan, and Sasha approaching. They wave, and I turn to Signy. She grins and winks.

"You didn't think I'd leave them out of your Stop Moping Day, did you?"

I chuckle as Dylan drags me from my seat and lifts me in a bear hug. The MMA fighter laughs.

"Feeling better after your baby sister had to cheer you up?"

I grab him in a headlock, and we tussle. Jagger, Tag, and Rust pile on until we're rolling around in the sand. The girls shout for them to stop teasing me and being bullies. Didn't I mention they love me the most?

When I break free, I give them hugs and swing them in the air despite growls from their mates. We settle at the table with Rust and Natalie on the edge of the sunbed. The server appears with platters of food instead of the plates I expected. Obviously, they planned this. We dig in and enjoy each other's company for the rest of the day, then change and party at Club Hati later that night.

The next morning, I awake to my usual routine—roll over and smile at Pillow Maya, sit up and study her photos on the nightstand, then open my email for Google alerts.

The joyful reprieve from the day before dissipates.

Maya Alejandra Perez Garcia Engaged to Emerico Tonio Santana Rodriguez

The Ultimate Merger of a Petroleum Conglomerate

Emerico Tonio Santana Rodriguez Claims the Prized Caraquenian Socialite Maya Alejandra Perez Garcia

Maya Alejandra Perez Garcia Is All Smiles For Her New Fiancé

I click dozens of headlines. As each article blathers on about the happy couple, my wolf's rage increases. My skin feels too tight and can't contain him. I will him to stand down. I won't have another break like I did at Tag's mansion. Taking a deep breath, I return to the websites and study Maya's face for any sign she truly wants the fucker.

Even though she smiles, her eyes remain distant. The closer I look, I notice her body language speaks louder than the headlines. He may have his arm around her waist —*grrrr*—but she angles away from him. In another photo, her hand rests stiffly on his arm. Yet in another where they dance, the camera catches a frown on her face hidden from his view. She's not the glowing bride-to-be the articles profess.

Signy's words come back to mind: *She's not married yet and deserves the right to know what fate plans for her.*

And she will.

~

Maya

"Oh, Maya! Look at all the coverage of your engagement party! It's international news, darling! Your father is so pleased. Our stock increased overnight in anticipation of the merger with Emerico's company…"

Roaring in my ears drown out my mother's voice as she goes on and on. The tablet she placed in front of me on the breakfast table blurs, then all goes dark.

"—passed out. I don't know what happened. Perhaps it's nerves?"

I crack one eye open despite my head beating like a bass drum. The pale yellow walls with paintings hung on them let me know I'm on the sofa in my mother's sitting room. A servant must have carried me here. I groan as a wave of nausea hits me.

"She's awake. Let me go."

My mother's heels click on the tile floor. The sweet scent of her perfume worsens the unease roiling in my belly.

I roll to my side with one hand cradling my head and the other my stomach. A wave of dizziness forces me onto my back again. A pitiful moan slips past my parted lips as my eyes close.

"Maya, don't move. You fainted at the table. Rest. I'll ring for some tea."

I listen as she speaks to the butler, who leaves the room for the kitchen. My mother returns and sits on a chair.

"You look pale. How do you feel?" She asks as she places the back of her hand on my forehead. "No fever. Do you hurt anywhere?"

"My head and stomach," I manage to respond as I hold back a gag from her perfume. "*Mamá*, no offense. But your perfume is too much for me."

She huffs and rises.

"Well, then. I'll wait over there, or shall I leave my sitting room?"

I groan at the bite of irritation in her voice.

"Never mind," I mumble.

The butler returns with a tray and pours tea. Roused by the aroma of peppermint, I sit up. The first sip soothes my belly. I sigh, thankful for the relief.

"As I said before you fainted, the reaction to your engagement pleases your father. In fact, Emerico called to join us for dinner. He wants to go over the timing for the wedding. I suggest a year for enough time to prepare and for your gown to be made. He's more inclined to six months. It seems he's eager for an heir..."

And then the tea tastes like bile.

However, I will myself to make it through the day.

Idania arrives, and my mother explains she will assist with the wedding preparations. Despite not having a firm date, she presses on. They schedule interviews for wedding planners the next day. Those selected will return with vision boards three days later. All are eager to snag what promises to be the wedding of the decade.

I do my best to match my mother's excitement. When she asks if I have any preference for colors or season, I respond in what I hope is an upbeat tone. She nods, pleased with my answers. She's even happier when I tell her I trust her vision and would rather she take the lead on the whole affair. Her hazel eyes shine as she beams.

"Wonderful, Maya! I think that's for the best. You focus on acquainting yourself with Emerico. I had Idania put together a dossier for you," she says and hands a binder to me. "She's gleaned the most important information about him. You study that and impress him with your knowledge. He'll appreciate a wife who knows him well and his preferences."

I take the binder and flip through it.

Photos, a family tree, relevant dates, favorite foods, clothing sizes… a complete dossier on Emerico Tonio Santana Rodriquez.

"Thank you, *Mamá*, Idania."

While they continue to chatter about the wedding, I read about the man I'm set to marry. He's not so bad. As far as an arranged marriage goes, it could be a hell of a lot worse. A man twice my age, boring, cruel, evil stepchildren. But he's still not Viggo. I sigh and flip the page. Best not to think about him.

My mother calls for a lunch break. But it's a continuation of the wedding preparation as she and Idania discuss ideas for the menu. I struggle to swallow past the lump in my throat.

We return to the sitting room, where they jump right back in. I study the dossier and respond to simple questions, including my preference for the gown shape. I say mermaid. My mother wants a ballgown. Uncaring, I give in.

At last, she calls an end to the day's preparation since she wants me well rested before dinner with Emerico. I glance down at my empty finger. He took the ring to resize it after he dropped me off at my apartment. More than likely, he'll have it tonight. And will happily slide it back on my finger.

Me not so much. Oh, well.

As expected, Emerico places the ring on my finger while we drink cocktails in my parents' living room. He leans in to kiss my lips. A slight tilt of my head as I pretend to admire the ring causes his lips land to on my cheek. I step back and hold my hand out to my mother. Her coos distract him from my slight. The beginnings of his scowl change into a grin as she exclaims how incredible the ring is. I smile more at the successful evasion than at the sparkler on my finger.

The butler announces dinner, and Emerico offers his arm. I slip my hand around it with a smile. No need to push too far so soon. My brothers take seats across the table from us while our parents sit at each head.

The conversation flows with my mother going straight to the wedding planning. I sit back sipping wine while she gushes on and on. Emerico glances at me from time to time. I nod and smile as though truly into it. I congratulate myself on an excellent performance.

"Well, Esmeralda, you and Maya have accomplished a lot in one day. I'm glad since I still prefer the wedding date in six months. We have the means to get all of Maya's wishes achieved by that time. Don't you agree, *bella*?"

I lift my wine and smile, "As you wish, Emerico."

He grins, and I tip the glass to my lips, draining it.

The countdown begins.

 iggo

"So, the playboy prince of the pack found his match, and now he wants to fly down to Venezuela to claim her?"

Jagger chuckles as he shakes his head and runs a hand through his white blond hair. Ice blue eyes sparkle with glee as we sit on the deck of his beachfront mansion on Moon Island. He lifts his snifter of Scotch and grins.

"I have to give it to you. You go from no interest to obsessed in a flash of a wolf shifter's eye. What are you going to do when you get there?"

I tell him Signy's suggestion and add, "Make her mine forever."

He cocks an eyebrow.

"Signy did not say to go that far. She said to let Maya

decide," he states, then raises a hand when I protest. "I get wanting to claim your fated mate desperately. Trust me, I've been there, bro. However, as your Alpha, I forbid you forcing her to mate. You will not issue the claiming bite without her permission. She must understand all it entails to transition into a she-wolf. But before you tell her anything, you must be sure she will not reveal us to other humans. Are we clear?"

And that's the thing. I have to tell Maya about what I am without exactly giving the full details. It will take time to feel her out. Anyone unaware of the paranormal world will either scoff at it, run scared, or rat us out. My hope is she will be open to it since her best friend is a she-wolf now.

"We're clear. I'll profess my love for her and ask her to return to Miami with me. Dump that fucker fiancé. I want to fly there now. But I know you need to speak with the local Alpha to get permission for me to enter his territory. Will you reach out now?"

Jagger studies me for a minute before he picks up his mobile.

I listen as he makes a few calls to get the Alpha's contact information. It takes a while since the South American wolf shifters are not members of our Ruling Council. But with their connections, Jagger gets the Alpha's mobile and email address. I wait as he calls.

I bite back a growl as I listen to Jagger's side of the conversation. They're on a pack run for the next week, and the Alpha doesn't want any wolf shifters in Caracas without him present. He'll call Jagger when they return.

"The good news is he gave you permission. In the meantime, come up with your strategy to win Maya's heart, lover boy."

He chuckles and sips his drink.

"Might I suggest you write a letter baring your soul to her?"

I turn on my chaise lounge to find Sage walking towards us with a charcuterie board of meats and cheeses. Jagger jumps to his feet to take it from her. Her emerald green eyes shine as she kisses his cheek and thanks him. His lopsided grin makes me laugh.

"Oh, so who's the lover boy, Jagger?"

He growls as he places the tray on the table, then purrs at Sage, pulling her onto his lap. She giggles and leans against him, then faces me.

"Signy and Wren told us girls all about your predicament, Viggo."

I groan and swipe a hand over my face. Leave it to Signy…

"Don't be embarrassed. You know you're our favorite"— she yelps when Jagger nips the mark from his claiming bite— "Don't be jealous, my love. We want Viggo to be happy too."

He grouses, and she pats his cheek before turning back to me.

"I met Maya at Club Hati the night you met, and we hung out at her going away party—"

"What going away party? Why didn't Wren tell me?"

Sage raises her hands palms up and shrugs.

"It was a Girls' Night Out. Sorry. But if it makes you feel any better, she didn't dance with any of the many guys who approached her."

I growl as my wolf snarls. Jealousy sparks through me as I envision some fucker grabbing her ass or gripping her hips. My vision tunnels—

"Now, now, Viggo, relax and listen to me."

I nod, knowing my voice will come out raspy with my wolf so close to the surface.

"I don't need my magick to sense Maya's attraction to you. When Signy mentioned your name just regarding the club, Maya's face lit up. She asked Signy about you. So, write a letter. Women adore love letters."

She tilts her head and smiles at Jagger. He grins and kisses her lips, murmuring words too low for me to pick up even with my enhanced hearing. She cuddles against him and nods at me.

"Thank you, Sage. That's a great idea, and I'll leave you two lovebirds to go write it now."

They wave as I stride around the house for my Harley on the driveway. There's only one place to inspire Maya's love letter. I turn right and ride a few doors from theirs. I roll onto the concrete-pavers driveway of the three-story glass and concrete modern mansion and hop off my bike.

A year ago, I built the residence for a future I imagined would include my family. I haven't spent the night yet. But this is where I will bring Maya. No way will I have her stay in my Ocean Drive penthouse with a bunch of horny bachelors. We'll make this our own home.

I enter through the oversized glass door and pause to admire the view of Biscayne Bay spread out past the open-concept great room. Its turquoise water glitters like the quartz flecks in the floor. Nothing covers it since I left it unfurnished, expecting my mate to want her touch on the place.

As I walk through the house, I make a mental note of items we'll need right away. I'll order a bed and linens for the primary suite, a sunbed and table for the deck, and floats for the pool. The one room I completed is the eat-in chef's kitchen, since I love to cook. Our first night home, I'll fix her a meal fit for a queen—my queen. With a grin, I add stocking the refrigerator and pantry to the list. Tour complete, I slide the accordion glass walls separating the great room from the outdoor living areas.

The infinity pool blends in with the bay for an expanse of azure waters. I strip out of my t-shirt, jeans, boxer briefs, socks, and boots, then dive in. The cool water sluices over my body as I swim a few laps. My mind wanders to thoughts of Maya and me skinny-dipping under the stars before I carry her to the side and ravish her sexy as fuck body.

My cock hardens, and I lift myself out and stretch out on the lawn. One arm bends behind my head while the other hand fists my dick. I close my eyes to a vision of Maya stepping from the pool with water dripping in rivulets down her golden skin. Hooded eyes caress my body, landing on my cock. Her full tits jiggle with each step. Narrow waist flares to grip-worthy hips, then tapers to long, toned legs. Her steps continue until she stands above me, feet planted on either side of my head.

I stare up into the pink paradise of her slick pussy. It's not only water dripping down her inner thighs. She's soaking wet. For. Me. My lips part and my tongue slips out as she lowers gracefully to her knees. I reach my hands up to grasp her hips, drawing her pussy down to my hungry mouth. A deep growl rumbles from my chest.

She shivers as my tongue traces her pussy lips. I tease her with several passes before I spear my tongue past her folds. The tip strokes her G-spot, and she cries out on a shudder. Her hands drop to the ground above my head as her hips gyrate.

I nip her inner thigh and growl.

"Be still! Only I give you pleasure."

She mewls and tenses her thigh muscles.

My mouth returns to her pussy for a feast. Tongue, teeth, fingers bring her to the edge again and again until she's a panting, dribbling mess. I lap at her juices, inhaling the fragrance of her musk mixed with her unique scent.

"Cum for me, my beauty. Cum for me now!"

My tongue wraps around her clit and sucks hard.

Her legs tremble as she cries out in Spanish. I smirk at her calling for her God.

"Not God, baby. Viggo—your fated mate."

Her pussy gushes.

I roar as my cock shoots ropes of jizz in the air. It dribbles down my hand and onto my eight-pack abs. My hips pump as my fist keeps a tight hold to coax every bit from my heavy balls. Spent, I sag into the grass as Maya's name slips from my lips.

Soon I will spill my seed inside of you. No condom at all.

Once my body recovers, I wash off in the outdoor shower, then add towels to the list… I sit on the grass to let the sun dry my body while I write the letter to Maya. A grin spreads across my face as I type it out on my mobile's note app. It doesn't take long since I don't hold back. I let my thoughts flow. Satisfied, I close the notes and pull up my contacts.

If I can't get to Maya for a week, I need eyes on her at all times. After a few calls, I connect with a human surveillance team who can have boots on the ground in Caracas tomorrow morning. They'll use their system to track her and have men watching her around the clock. They'll report on her every move, and if she's in trouble, they'll step in.

They're not me. But it's better to have some idea of what's going on aside from Google alerts.

I sit and watch the activity on the bay while my mind wanders. After a while, I dress and ride back to Ocean Drive. A couple of males get on the elevator discussing their latest conquests in lewd detail. I roll my eyes. Yeah, this is not the place for Maya.

My fully furnished penthouse feels emptier than the mansion with nothing in it. I sigh as I head to my bedroom suite. Then grin as I think about how I'll have Maya home soon. My wolf grins with his tongue lolling from the side of his mouth. For the first time in weeks, we agree.

Maya

"Hey! I was just thinking about you! How's everything going?"

Wren's smiling face appears on my mobile when she accepts my FaceTime video call. But her smile fades as she peers closer at me.

"Maya, what's wrong? You don't look so good, honey. Are you ill?"

The tears I've been holding all day spill down my cheeks as a sob bursts from my chest. It heaves as I let it all out. Wren waits patiently, offering words of comfort until I get a hold of myself. I wipe my face with a tissue and pick up the mobile.

"My period is late."

Wren's gasp makes me cry anew.

"Oh, Maya! I'm so sorry. I didn't mean to make you cry. Let's think this through. Okay?"

I snuffle and nod.

"How late are you? And are you always regular?"

"A week and yes," I wail.

"Okay. Oaky. Um… Let me look up the symptoms."

She types away on her mobile while I try to get it together.

"Okay, let me know if you experience any of these... metallic taste in your mouth, nausea, sore breasts?"

"Yes, to all. Oh, Wren! What am I going to do if I'm pregnant? My parents will have a fit, and Emerico... I don't know! *Ay Dios mío...*"

Wren's silence makes me look at the mobile screen. She bites her lower lip with her eyebrows furrowed. I know that look, and I won't like what she's about to say.

"Um... You should tell Vi—"

"No! I'm not ready to tell anyone but you, Wren. I mean it! Do not tell Viggo or Tag. Promise me!"

Her eyes widen as she stares at me for a moment. Then she nods slowly.

"I promise. It'll be hard since Tag reads me like a book" —she raises her hand when I cry out—"But I won't give in. You're my best friend, and it's your body, your decision. I support you completely. You need to go to the doctor for confirmation. For all we know, it's just nerves about your wedding messing with your hormones. You won't be the first bride-to-be who misses a period because of stress."

That hadn't occurred to me. My stomach unclenches as I sigh in relief.

"Yes! Yes! That's it, Wren. You're so smart, chica! I'll make an appointment with my doctor. Hopefully she can see me tomorrow. Let me go so I can call. I'll call you back."

We end the FaceTime, and I call my doctor's office. I say a prayer of thanks when her secretary offers an afternoon time. It's perfect since it won't coincide with the caterer's meeting. I'll make an excuse to leave my mother and go see the doctor.

I cling to Wren's thought of stress's impact on hormones. It's a likely cause. Not the broken condom and Viggo's super sperm. At least that's what I tell myself…

I call Wren back. She tries to take my mind off the situation by asking me about the wedding until I grimace. She changes tactics and asks when she can come to visit. That perks me up, and we make plans for her to come in a couple of weeks.

Later that night, I dream of wolves running amongst pine trees and high grasses of a marsh. A pup yips as it chases a butterfly in a patch of wildflowers. For the first time in weeks, I wake rested with a smile on my face.

Then I remember my appointment and tears well in my eyes.

Maya, you are so screwed and not in the right way, chica!

Somehow, I make it through the day's wedding preparation itinerary and escape with the excuse of going to the gym. My mother thinks it's a great idea to keep fit for Emerico. I exchange an eye roll with a forced smile before I kiss her cheeks and hurry from the caterer's kitchen.

During the cab ride, I stare out the window, lost in thought. If I'm not pregnant, great. If I am, well, I'll have to tell Viggo at some point. But I won't depend upon him to raise my baby. However, since he's in Miami, my parents will probably not want to see me for a while, and to avoid the press, I'll move back to my second home. At least I'll have the love and support of my best friend.

My mobile chirps with a text message. A smile appears on my face at Wren's name on the screen.

No matter what, we're in this together! I love you! Call me with news.

Tears fill my eyes as I respond with a smiley face emoticon. My hands shake too much for more typing. I return the mobile to my handbag just as the cab stops in front of my doctor's office. I take a deep breath and pay the fare before I step out to face my fate.

 aya

You're pregnant, Maya.

My doctor's words reverberate in my head as I sit in the waiting room of the OB-GYN she recommended. Since the doctor is popular with socialites, I was afraid to come for fear word would leak before I can speak with my family and Emerico. But she's the best in the city, and I will provide the best for my baby. But I keep my sunglasses on for a bit of anonymity.

"*Señorita?*"

I jolt when a nurse appears next to me. She smiles.

"The doctor will see you now. Kindly follow me."

I gather my handbag and mobile, then follow her down a hallway lined with photos of newborn babies and ecstatic parents. My heart clenches as I wonder if Viggo will be elated or pissed. We were only in it for the one night, nothing more. Now, I'm pregnant. How could I know my steamy act of rebellion would result in a surprise?

The nurse stops by the open door of an examination room and gestures for me to enter. Frozen, my gaze flicks between the table with stirrups and the ultrasound machine. I startle when the nurse calls my name. She smiles again.

"Kindly change into the gown behind the door. The doctor will be with you shortly."

I nod mutely and enter the room.

I shiver as the cold air wraps around my bare skin. The thin cotton gown does little to warm me as I perch on the edge of the examination table. My unfocused eyes stare at the wall where more photos hang. The colorful images blur into a kaleidoscope, making me dizzy. A polite cough draws my attention from the wall to the door. I blink.

"Hello, Maya, I'm Dr. Morillo. It's a pleasure to meet you. I understand your doctor confirmed you're pregnant and you would like me to provide a full examination?"

"Yes."

"Well, let's get started."

She proceeds to exam me, then checks the file and frowns. Alarmed, I sit up.

"W—What's the matter? Is something wrong?"

"Ah… this is the file your doctor sent with the numbers from your hCG test. Your hormone levels are much higher than expected at this stage. Are you certain you conceived only five weeks ago?"

I blink in confusion and count back, then nod.

"Absolutely. I remember the morning the condom broke. Five weeks ago."

She nods and smiles.

"I'm sure it's nothing to be concerned about. Errors can occur. I suggest you retake the test now."

I slide from the exam table and walk to the en suite bathroom. My heart pounds as I complete the sample. I leave it on the sink for the nurse.

She takes it and disappears while the doctor makes notes. The nurse returns, and the doctor scans the new numbers. The frown returns. My heart skips a beat as I place a protective hand on my slightly rounded belly.

"Well, these numbers coincide with the original ones. Normally, this level would indicate a pregnancy at the eleven-weeks mark. Interesting. But we will proceed based on your five weeks..."

I attempt to concentrate on her words about supplements, nutrition, and appointments. But my mind sticks on the different hormone levels. Why?

"Should I be concerned?" I ask, interrupting her sentence.

She pauses and considers me before she responds.

"Based on the rest of your exam and numbers, you're an extremely healthy young woman. It's obvious you take great care of yourself," she says and smiles reassuringly. "Each woman's body varies. I see no other issues. So, do not worry. You don't want to stress yourself or your baby."

I study her face for any sign of an untruth. Finding none, I nod and refocus on her recommendations. I don't mention my return to Miami. Instead, I tell her I'll have to check my calendar before I schedule the follow-up visits. By the time I leave, I feel a bit better but exhausted.

As I walk through the front doors, the sidewalk tilts and my vision darkens on the edges until only pinpoints of light remain. As everything goes black, a woman's scream is the last thing I hear.

"*Señorita?*"

My eyes open to a stranger's face. The top half covered by aviator sunglasses prevent me from seeing his eyes. But concern fills his voice. Held in his arms as he kneels on the ground, I glance around.

Others gathered around us, stare and point. A camera clicks. The flash blinds me. I close my eyes to block the glare as white bursts dance before them. The man curses at the photographer but doesn't let me go. I clutch his arm and sit up.

"I—I'm fine. Thank you. I'll get a cab now."

His attention returns to me. He studies my face, then nods and rises, lifting me with him. I tighten my grip on his arm as I wobble on my heels.

"Careful, *señorita*. I've got you. Let me get you in a cab. You need to get home and rest."

I mumble in agreement as he guides me to the sidewalk. A cab waits at the curb. He opens the door and helps me inside. He and the driver exchange a glance and a nod. I tilt my head, thinking the driver seems familiar. He pushes his sunglasses up and faces forward.

"*¿Adónde, señorita?*"

I give him the address to my apartment and settle back in the seat. The stranger smiles and pats my arm. Before he closes the door, he tells me to take care of myself and my baby. Surprised, I stare at him. He points to the doctor's office and smiles as he shuts the door. Of course, the gold plaque by the entry displays the doctor's name and practice. I place a hand on my belly and offer him a weary smile, then close my eyes.

"*Nosotras estamos aqui senorita.*"

My eyes open, and I glance out the window to find we arrived at my building. The doorman steps forward as I pay the fare. Again, I study the driver. He thanks me and averts his face as he checks the side-view mirror. I shake my head and step out of the cab.

Once inside my apartment, I shower and slip into a cashmere v-neck lounge dress. A bit of nausea leads me to the kitchen for a cup of peppermint tea and some crackers I started keeping in stock. Curled on the sofa, I FaceTime Wren. She answers on the first ring. Her worried face fills the screen.

"Well?"

"I'm pregnant."

Her lips press together as she nods.

"Okay. Is everything all right? Nothing odd?"

My breath hitches.

"Tell me!"

"The doctor says my hormone levels are higher than normal for five weeks, more like eleven. She told me not to worry. But it scares me. What if something's wrong with my baby? I couldn't bear it!"

Wren shakes her head vigorously.

"It's okay, trust me. Don't you worry at all. And do not stress yourself out, promise?"

I nod, and she continues.

"Take tonight to rest and adjust to the news. Don't make any decisions or say anything to anyone until we talk tomorrow. You look tired, no offense. Go take a nap. Okay?"

I nod and end the call. Pressing my hand to my lower belly, I lower to my side and let my eyes drift shut. Tomorrow. Tomorrow, I'll decide what to do. Once again, wolves fill my dreams. But this time, Viggo leads them.

Viggo

"WHAT?!?!?!"

I growl and jump to my feet as my guy in Caracas tells me Maya fainted outside of an OB-GYN's office. My wolf snarls and bares his fangs, pacing at the edges of my being. I listen as the human tells me all the details he gleaned. They checked the doctor's digital files but didn't see one for Maya yet. They'll get back to me once they have it.

But I don't need him to tell me anything.

Maya is pregnant with my pup.

She hasn't been in Caracas long enough to be pregnant by that fucker. My stomach churns at the thought of him even touching her and to have sex? Hell to the no!

Mine!

I end the call and dial Jagger.

"Maya's pregnant with my pup. I must get to her now. Right now, fly from Miami to Caracas. I will not wait for that Alpha. It's been a week, and he should've called by now. Well, too fucking late. I'm out!"

"Hold on. Let me call him right now. You call the pilot to get a jet ready."

I end the call and get on the line with our pack's pilot. He promises to ready the flight plan for no later than an hour. I'll take a helicopter to Miami International and get there in ten minutes. While I rush upstairs to pack a bag, Jagger calls to confirm the Alpha returned and is aware I'm on my way. As if I cared. Maya needs me and nothing and no one will keep me from her and my pup.

My Harley zips to Moon Island's helipad. I leave the bike in the hangar and race to climb aboard the helicopter.

"Okay, let's go. Let's go!"

The pilot nods but doesn't take off.

"What's up? We gotta go!"

The door slides open. Jagger hops in, followed by Wren, Tag, Rust, and Dylan.

My mouth drops.

"You know I can't have my younger brother go to another pack's territory to get his fated mate without me."

"Damn right!"

"Hell, yeah, bro!"

"You can't go anywhere without backup, Viggo."

"And Maya is my best friend. She needs me too!"

I grin as they settle in the leather captain chairs and tighten their seatbelts.

Wren pats my arm and smiles.

"I'm glad you're going to get Maya, Viggo. She's so scared—"

"You spoke to her? You already knew and didn't tell me?"

Tag growls and leans around Wren.

"Back the fuck up, Viggo. Wren didn't tell me either, and I'm her mate."

She shakes her head.

"I promised Maya I wouldn't say a word to anyone, including Tag. She wanted to confirm her guess and time to think about her next steps—"

"Next steps! She's coming home, and that's final."

Wren flares her nostrils as Jagger growls. His Alpha command hits me in the chest like a sledgehammer. I fall back in my seat.

"Nothing is final, Viggo. I told you Maya must give you permission. Do not disobey me. I will not warn you again."

Tension flares, but I back down to his will.

Rust clears his throat.

"As the pack doctor and mate to the pack OB-GYN, I cannot allow you to issue a claiming bite while Maya is pregnant. She is human. We do not know how her body will react to the transition under normal circumstances. Being pregnant ups the risks to her and to the pup. You will wait until after she gives birth."

My stomach flips.

I forgot about the whole human aspect. Dammit! I was wary before. Now, I'm scared as fuck. I drop my head to my hands and lean my elbows on my thighs. This is more than I expected.

"It's going to be all right, Viggo," Wren says as she pats my back. "Maya is a strong woman. But don't push her. Let her decide her next steps. I truly doubt she'll leave you out of them."

I nod and sit back, staring out the window. MIA appears in the distance. Soon we'll touch down in Caracas, and I can hold Maya in my arms. I'll give her all the love she needs. But I won't let her tell me no. No matter what Jagger and the others say, I will bring Maya home to Miami, and we will be together.

And if that fucker tries anything, I'll rip his head off.

We board the private jet, and the pilot confirms we'll land in a little over three hours. Shortly after takeoff, my mobile vibrates with an email. My pulse quickens at the sight of Maya's OB-GYN file. I scan the notes and her concern about the hormone levels. Fuck!

"Rust, I need you to take a look at this," I say as I sit on a chair across from him stretched out on a sofa. "It's Maya's medical file. Tell me what the hormone levels mean. The doctor is curious about them. We don't need her to get nosy and stir up shit. That won't be good for any of us."

"Damn," he says as he swings his long legs around and takes my mobile. He reads through the file and nods. "Well, I wouldn't worry about it. Maya's body is adjusting to a wolf shifter pup. She won't have human ranges for anything. We don't have a point of reference since the few humans turned she-wolves transitioned before they became pregnant. My guess is Maya will deliver sooner than nine months. By this rate, I'd say in six or so. Natalie will exam her and run tests if Maya comes back with us. If not, I'll see what I can do down there."

He glances at Jagger and calls him over.

"Listen, Viggo has Maya's medical record, and the doctor has questions about the numbers. You need to be aware since we may need to delete Maya's records. We don't need any info lingering that humans can study. They did bloodwork too. We'll erase everything."

"Fuck! All the more reason for you to persuade Maya to return to Miami. I investigated her fiancé. He will not be happy since their marriage included the merger of his and her family's companies. The stocks have already increased. No one will be happy, least of all them. I'd say offer a bride-price if they put up a stink. We'll go back to Viking times for that one, bro. As long as she agrees."

My nostrils flare at the last bit, and Jagger cocks an eyebrow. I sigh and take my mobile from Rust, then return to my chair.

They leave me alone while I stare out the window, mind racing. I'm certain Maya will return with me, especially once I tell her how I feel. But I'll wait to tell her about being a wolf shifter until after she gets to Miami. I don't want to scare her off. Then I'll have to really go back to Viking times and kidnap her. Jagger will lose his shit. I say a prayer to the gods since this was their bright idea and hope Maya will come of her own free will.

Regardless, she. Is. Mine.

We land, and I send a message to my guy as we ride in Suburbans to a hotel near Maya's apartment building. I want to be as close to her as possible and booked rooms while on board the jet. My guy will meet us there with the latest news.

Jagger confirms the local Alpha will stop by to meet him and help where he can.

At the hotel, we stride in like we own the place. The staff at the reception desk perks up and checks us in without delay. Jagger, Tag, Wren, and I take the three-bedroom President's Suite while Rust and Dylan stay in two surrounding suites.

I pace the floor while we wait for the Alpha and my guy to arrive. The Alpha arrives first, and Jagger makes the introductions.

"Alpha, we appreciate you giving permission for us to enter your territory. As I mentioned, Viggo's fated mate is a human—Maya Alejandra Perez Garcia. You may know her family."

"Of course. Very influential in Venezuela. I read she's

engaged to Emerico Tonio Santana Rodriguez, another prominent businessman. You say she's your fated mate, Viggo?"

"Absolutely. She bears the scent I first inhaled as a newborn pup. Maya is mine. I do not give a damn about Rodriguez or his prominence. She's also pregnant with my pup, not that it's your concern. I'm doubly invested in bringing her back to Miami."

He nods.

"Fine. You have my full support. Contact me if you need any help. Good luck, my friend."

The Alpha extends his hand, and we shake. He continues the gesture with the others before Jagger walks him to the door. He returns with my guy, and we sit around the dining room table.

"What's the latest? Is she still at home?"

He goes on to tell us Maya hasn't left her apartment since one of his men drove her home. He and another alternate as cab drivers as they follow her. If she's not with her mother and needs a cab, they pull up before anyone else. It's a suitable cover. Others follow in cars and trail her on foot when she goes somewhere. They have a handle on her routine.

When I ask when she's likely to be alone, he tells us she hikes in the park every other morning. Tomorrow is the next expected day. He provides details, and we plan to follow her until she's deep enough inside I can approach her without being seen. Wren will remain at the hotel, despite her protest.

That night, I toss and turn in bed, unable to sleep as my mind and wolf run wild. When I doze off, Maya fills my dreams. Her smiling face stares at me until the sunlight filters through the sheer curtains. I jump up and stare at the silver-framed photo I brought with me.

Soon, you will be in my arms. Forever.

CHAPTER 10

$\mathcal{M}$aya

EACH TIME I hike in Waraira Repano National Park, it brings me solace. Before it was for the arranged marriage and losing the life I wanted to live in Miami. Today, it has an additional benefit. Being in nature, surrounded by the abundance of life, reminds me of the baby growing in my womb. A new life dependent upon me for nourishment, protection, and most of all, for love.

My heart swells with joy for my little one. The unexpected consequence of my decision to live as I want before resigning myself to Emerico may upend my world. But my baby is my *Pequeño Tesoro* and I will cherish my little treasure always.

The first smile since the doctors confirmed my pregnancy spreads across my face. I place both hands on my lower belly. It's more pronounced than yesterday, as though overnight my baby decided it would show the world it exists. Worry makes my smile falter. Perhaps there's more to the abnormal hormones than the doctors believe. *Stop it, Maya.* I push the negative thoughts away and continue along the trail.

The sound of rushing water quickens my pace. I can't wait to take a dip in the refreshing waters, a cleansing for my spirit. I step past the trees and onto the grass surrounding the waterfall's crystal-clear pool. Sunlight sparkles like diamonds on its surface.

Eager to cool off from the long hike, I lower my backpack to the ground and lift the hem of my tank top. As it covers my face, a menacing growl sounds behind me. I spin as my hands drop the tank top back in place. But the image before me makes me wish I couldn't see its beady eyes and mouth gaping with teeth as long as my fingers. It shakes its giant head. Saliva drips from its fangs.

Fear freezes me to the spot. My heart races as I watch the bear rise to its hind legs. Paws the size of skillets tipped with black claws swing in the air. A vision of them ripping into my belly jolts me from the trance. I glance around for anything I can use as a weapon to protect my baby. A thick branch lies a few feet to my left. I decide to dart right to trick it to run in that direction so I can double back and pick up the branch.

Howls fill the air.

I stop with one foot raised. The hairs on the back of my neck rise as a tingle spreads through my body. My eyes shift from the bear to the trees behind it. Five massive wolves break from the brush and charge the bear. Their mouths are wide with fangs just as lethal snap. The bear lumbers to turn towards his foes. The wolves circle it. A red and white one rush between the bear and me. Their heads reach my shoulders, leaving only the top of the bear in my view.

I back away towards the branch, keeping my eyes on the scene. Better for me to have a means to defend myself than to stand here and get slaughtered. But by which of the beasts?

Once my fingers wrap around the thick tree limb, I hold it in front of me like a bat. My head swivels as I seek an escape route. But the only clear path is the trail, and the beasts block it. The pool offers no shelter, and the surrounding dense vegetation prevents a clear pass.

A roar of pain captures my attention.

The black wolf clings to the bear's back. Its jaws clamp around the thick neck. The bear reaches around. But the brown wolf and the second red one sink their fangs into the bear's front legs as they flail. The white wolf leaps onto the bear's chest. Its claws dig into the bear's shoulders and rear legs before it roars and rips the bear's throat out. A gurgling growl marks the end of the bear. It collapses to the ground. Blood seeps from multiple wounds and gushes from its ravaged neck. The wolves throw their heads back and howl.

Bile rises in my throat. I brace myself on the tree branch and retch.

"Maya."

Hands clasp my waist and pull me flush against a muscular body—a naked, muscular body. I scream and bash the branch on the back. The body doesn't flinch. The hands tighten their grip.

"Maya, it's me, Viggo."

My eyes focus on the chest in front of me. The familiar wolf paws on the pecs surprise me. My gaze lifts up and up until it settles on his face, streaked with dirt and blood. His fiery copper red hair is wild around his head. The tattoos on his scalp stand out even more. I gasp and struggle to free myself from his vise-like grip.

"How are you here? Why do you have blood on your face?" I ask then I remember the bear and the wolves. I try to peek around his wide chest. "Wh—Where are the bear and the wolves?"

He swallows audibly then takes a deep breath.

"The bear can't hurt you. It's dead. I'm one wolf, as are Tag, you know, and my brother Jagger, Rust, and Dylan."

My eyes dart over his face. Not wanting to believe him. Impossible! How the hell can they be wolves?! I may not know his brother and the other two. But I've been around Tag dozens of times. He's no wolf!

"He is, as are the rest of us. Trust me, Maya."

I blink. Did I speak aloud?

Viggo nods at my spoken thoughts again.

"Maya, I will explain all to you. But first we need to get

rid of the bear before anyone comes along. I'm going to rinse off in the water. You stay right here."

When he moves to the side, I peer around him. The four wolves sit beside the bear. They watch me. I gape at them.

"Tag?"

The brown wolf stands. I jump back and stumble on a rock. Quick as a flash, Viggo grabs me.

"Careful, Maya! They won't hurt you. Neither will I. Let me rinse off."

My mouth opens and closes like a fish. I give up on a verbal response and shake my head. This isn't real. I must be dreaming like I did weeks ago when the red wolf appeared here. Red wolf??? My head swings to Viggo who stands waist deep in the water, watching me as he washes the grime off.

"Are you the red wolf?"

"Yes."

My knees give way. But before I crumple to the ground, Viggo catches me.

He bends down and presses his forehead to mine.

"I didn't expect to tell you this way. But it'll be okay, Maya. I promise. Trust me, my love. Please."

I don't know what to say, so I remain silent. Then another thought occurs to me.

"Wren! Does she know?"

The brown wolf chuffs. My gaze whips to him. He nods his head and chuffs again. I gasp and cling to Viggo to stop from dropping to the ground. He holds me tighter.

"Come. I need my backpack to put on some clothes.

We'll head down the trail while the others handle the bear. They'll catch up to us," he says as he picks up my backpack and wraps an arm around my waist, tucking me into his side.

I don't want to think about how they'll *handle the bear*, or about them being wolves, or about Wren knowing and not telling me. I don't want to think at all. Instead, I nod and let him guide me from the clearing, giving the dead bear and humongous wolves a wide berth.

I close my eyes as we pass them. The stench of blood and gore roils my stomach. I whimper and pull against Viggo's grip. He loosens his hold when he realizes I'm sick.

"Oh, Maya, I'm sorry. But we couldn't let the bear harm you," he says as he holds my ponytail away from my face.

My body relaxes as a deep rumbling wraps around me like a soothing weighted blanket. When I straighten, I notice the sound comes from Viggo. It vibrates from his chest, straight to my soul. Tears fill my eyes as I wrap my arms around his waist and press my face into his chest. His heart beats strong beneath my forehead. My eyes close as I sob.

So much happened in the last few weeks. My mind needs a rest.

Viggo scoops me up and carries me past the trees. He sets me down while he puts on his clothes, then lifts me into his arms again. I protest when he turns down the path.

"Viggo, it's too far for you to carry me. I can walk."

He shakes his head as fierce determination shines in his ice blue eyes.

"Maya, you and my pup are mine to care for, protect, and to love. Forever. You rest. I'm here now. We will never be apart again."

Tears threaten until my mind replays his words.

"Your p—pup?"

He nods and glances at my belly. The tank top fails to hide the noticeable bump.

"I know you're pregnant—"

"Did Wren tell you?!"

"No. Your scent changed. There's a fainter one blended with yours."

I blink.

Of course, he can detect smells. He's a damn wolf!

"Wait! You said 'pup.' Is my baby a wolf too? Will I give birth to a wolf?!"

"I don't believe so—"

"You 'don't believe so?' What the hell does that mean? Don't you know? You're a wolf! You should know!"

"Maya, please calm down. You're upsetting yourself and my pup. I'll explain everything when we get to the hotel."

The possibility I'm hurting my baby makes me close my mouth and my eyes. I visualize an infinity pool extending to azure waters. A gentle breeze casts ripples across both. *Peace and tranquility. Peace and tranquility.* I repeat the mantra timed to my breaths, releasing my mind in meditation. I relax against Viggo with hands on my belly.

"Maya, we're near the parking lot."

Viggo's soft murmur in my ear brings me to my surroundings.

"I need you to promise me you won't say anything to anyone about what happened with the bear and, most importantly, about us being wolf shifters. Humans will experiment on us and hunt us into extinction, as has happened in the past. Promise me."

I pause to consider. But the impassioned expression in his eyes and the fact I'm carrying a wolf shifter baby-pup set my decision.

"I promise, Viggo. I can't have anything happen to my baby."

A flash of hurt crosses his face. Oops. I didn't mention him.

I cup his cheek.

"Or to you."

He closes his eyes and inhales deeply as he nuzzles against my palm. My heart clenches. Truly, I couldn't stand it if something happened to him.

"Thank you," he says, then cocks his head. "The others are right behind us. Let's get you in the SUV."

He strides across the parking lot.

A man hops out of the driver's seat. I gasp.

"You! You're the man who helped me yesterday."

He bows his head, and I swing my gaze to Viggo.

"Did you have me followed?"

The fierce determination reappears as he lifts his chin.

"Absolutely. I couldn't get down here for a week, and I needed to be sure you were safe."

I should be angry he invaded my privacy. But the part of me that yearns for support—not to mention the renewed need for him—warms to his possessiveness. I cup his cheek again and smile.

"Okay, okay."

His eyes light up as he grins. The man opens the SUV's door, and Viggo places me on the middle of the first row. He puts my backpack on my lap before he shuts the door. I watch as he talks to Tag and the others, I guess to be the wolves. They're all huge, well over six feet, and muscular. I thought Viggo resembled a Viking warrior. The others do too.

They pile into the SUV, smiling at me. Tag gets in last and sits beside me.

"Hiya, Maya," he says and chuckles.

I'm surprised the serious man can crack a joke. I grin and shake my head.

"Hi, Tag. Fancy seeing you here."

The one with the white blond hair turns around from the passenger seat and smiles at me.

"I'm Jagger, Viggo's brother. It's a pleasure to meet you at last."

I return his smile and thank him.

The others introduce themselves as Dylan and Rust. I recall which wolf did what damage to the bear. It's still hard to believe. But here they are, and the bear? Well, *handled.*

We ride to the hotel in silence while Viggo holds my hand on his thigh. He squeezes it when we pull up to the entrance. I nod and take a deep breath. Soon I'll have answers.

However, the question is, am I ready?

~

Viggo

MY HEART nearly burst from my chest when the bear appeared ahead of us on the path. His growl confirmed he spied Maya. Without hesitation, we dropped our backpacks and shifted, rending our clothes as our wolves leaped forth. As a pack, we charged. Instinctively, I put myself between the bear and my fated mate. Jagger bounded beside me. The others circled him, preventing his escape.

My only thought was to protect Maya. Each of us took turns attacking the bear until Jagger issued the death bite. Immediately, I shifted and rushed to her side. My heart clenched as she threw up. Arms held her close, needing to wrap her up in safety.

I'm thankful she didn't fight me too much. But now that we're in the hotel, I hope she'll remain open to what I have to tell her.

The door to the President's Suite opens as we walk down the hallway. Wren races out, arms outstretched.

"Maya! Thank the gods you're fine!"

Her head jerks up in surprise to find her best friend here. Then she hurries towards her. They embrace with joyous cries. Tag and I usher them into the suite while the others follow.

"Wren! Why didn't you tell me?!"

A sheepish expression appears on her face as her eyes dart to Jagger and Tag. Our Alpha speaks.

"Maya, do not be upset with Wren. No one may speak of our kind to humans. Allow Viggo to explain all to you. We'll wait in the living room."

He nods at me.

I step forward and place a hand on Maya's lower back. I guide her to the library and shut the door. She sits when I gesture at the sofa. I perch on the coffee table and place my hands on her thighs between mine. My eyes go to her rounded belly. Pride swells in my chest. My pup. I lift my gaze to her face. My mate. Mine!

"Maya, I want to start by saying I missed you the moment you stepped out of Club Hati. The need to be with you was strong. I lost my shit when I saw your farewell video post. I ran to find you. But you were gone. When Wren told me you left for an arranged marriage, the pain was so great I shifted and rampaged for hours. The only reason I didn't come for you then was my concern for you as a human and what it means to be a wolf shifter."

Tears slip down her cheeks as I speak. My fingertips brush them away.

I can't resist the urge to kiss her. She doesn't pull away when I lean in slowly, giving her enough time to deny me. Our lips touch, and lights flash behind my closed eyelids. Electricity zings from our locked mouths along my jaw and down to my heart. It pumps faster as the kiss deepens.

She mewls, and I groan.

My hands glide along the outside of her thighs to grip her hips. They dig into her flesh. She scoots forward. I growl and move over her, turning and pressing her into the sofa. My erect cock tents the joggers. The tip nudges her pussy, hidden by shorts. Her hips lift and knees fall apart to welcome me. I don't hesitate.

In seconds, we're naked. My cock bobs against my abs. I fist it and guide it to her pussy. Again, I move slowly, giving her the chance to say no. Instead, she moans and lifts her hips as her fingernails dig into my biceps and her ankles lock behind my ass.

My cock sinks inside her wet warmth, and we groan in unison as we meld as one. Fully bare with no condom or remnants of one. I take a moment to breathe before I spill my load as her pussy throbs around my dick.

"Viggo, please. I need you. So badly…"

Her hips undulate as her pussy sucks me deeper. I bottom out with my balls kissing the bottom curve of her ass. I place her hands above her head to brace them on the armrest. On either side of hers, I place mine. Planked above, I stare into her topaz eyes darkened to obsidian by her lust blown pupils. Her mouth hangs slack as she stares up at me.

"I need you more than you can imagine, my love. I'll take you hard now. Later, we'll make love."

Before her chin meets her chest in a nod of affirmation, my hips draw back and snap forward. Her elbows bend and fuller tits bounce as I drive her up the sofa. Her mouth opens in a silent scream. She sucks in air as I withdraw, then keens.

My mouth crashes to hers and swallows her carnal cries. Our tongues tangle as our pelvises collide in a frenzied, desperate need to connect. Her juices coat my cock, easing its way into her tight pussy. I growl as she clenches around me.

"Cum for me as many times as you need, baby. Cum hard for your mate!"

She keens as her pussy walls constrict. They quiver along my length as I slam into her with enough force to move her further up to the sofa. One hand lowers to cradle the top of her head to prevent it from hitting the armrest.

I rise to my toes, using my ass and thighs to power on. Skin slaps against skin as the scent of our fucking rises to fill my nostrils and to urge me faster. The sofa creaks in protest. But I don't slow. Not when my heavy balls draw up and electricity zings along the backs of my thighs to the base of my spine, and down my cock.

I pound Maya's pussy harder. My knot forms and locks behind her pussy wall. She screams and writhes beneath me as her fingernails claw the silk. It rips as she screams my name. My fangs elongate, dripping with serum. But Rust's warning not to issue the claiming bite while she's pregnant jumps to the forefront of my mind.

I yank my head back. With my wolf so close to the surface, a primal roar rips from my throat. Our bodies spasm as we climax together. My arms and legs give out. Before I crush her with my weight, I turn us to the side.

Nestled against me, she pants. Her sweat-dampened forehead presses to my neck.

"Viggo… what is that?"

I stroke her back and rumble to soothe her.

"My knot. It expands at the base of my cock to lock you to me while my seed travels to your womb. I didn't release it the first time we were together, even though I wanted to."

She mewls and whimpers as it stretches her pussy.

"It'll get better the more you get used to it. In about fifteen minutes, it'll deflate. Rest now, my love."

She snuggles closer, and our legs intertwine.

I continue to rumble until her breathing evens out. Once she's asleep, my eyes drift closed. Later. We'll talk later.

 aya

"Hello, my sleeping beauty."

My eyes open completely as I stretch languorously in the sumptuous sheets. Then I frown and sit up, glancing around. Viggo grins.

"I laid it on you so good, I knocked you out. A sofa is no place for a long nap. This is my room in the suite. If you're rested, I'll bathe you in the shower, and you'll eat before we talk."

"Mmmmm… sounds good," I purr as he scoops me from the bed. My arms wrap around his neck. A girl could get used to this treatment.

Not only does Viggo bathe me, but he also makes me cum on his tongue until my legs shake. He dries me and massages lotion into my skin. Then he carries me to the walk-in closet where he drops a silk caftan over my head. He dresses in a t-shirt and low-hanging joggers sans underwear. My mouth drools as he tucks away his delectable cock. He smirks when he catches my heated stare.

"Later. I heard your stomach growl as I dried you. Wren ordered your favorite foods. They're in the warming drawer. Come, time to feed you and my pup."

He scoops me up, and I grin.

"You spoil me, Viggo."

He shrugs his wide shoulders.

"What else am I supposed to do?"

We enter the living room to applause. My cheeks flush crimson. Without a doubt, they heard my screams. I duck my head against Viggo's neck. His shoulders shake as he chuckles.

"Aaaw! No need for embarrassment, Maya. Not much gets past our enhanced hearing. You'll see," Wren says.

"Hold on. You said, 'our enhanced hearing.' How is that?"

Wren opens, then closes her mouth as her eyes flick between Viggo and me. He shakes his head.

"We were a bit too busy to talk. Let me get her and my pup fed. Why don't you join us in the dining room?"

He strides through the living room without waiting for an answer. In the dining room, he settles me in a chair and goes to the kitchenette.

Wren and the others trail in. She sits next to me and smiles.

"Tell—"

"Nope. Not a word about anything until you've eaten some food," Viggo interrupts as he returns with a tray loaded with platters. He sits on my other side and places the tray in front of me. As he puts a selection of meats on a plate, he continues. "You'll need loads of protein. Right, Rust?"

"Yes. And don't let it alarm you if you crave less cooked meat," he winks as my eyes widen. "Not to freak you out or anything."

Wren pats my arm and smiles.

The thought of consuming raw meat makes me think of the bear. But instead of nausea, my mouth waters. What the heck? *Ay Dios mío!*

While I eat, the conversation flows easily. As Viggo commanded, no one mentions wolves, pups, or anything related. When I finish two plates, he grins and strokes my belly.

"Nice and full, my little one?"

Everyone laughs.

Rust and Dylan clear the table while the rest of us return to the living room. Viggo puts me on his lap, and I snuggle happily in his arms. Tag does the same with Wren, and we smile at one another. Jagger sits beside Viggo and looks at him expectantly. Viggo nods.

I listen in awe about the history of wolf shifters and their pack's arrival in what's now Miami so long ago. The notion of other paranormal beings intrigues me, especially learning Sage is the High Witch, the most powerful of all. I realize folklore holds some truths. I just never thought I would be in the middle of one. And definitely not pregnant with a half human wolf shifter pup!

However, concern rises when Viggo tells me about the claiming bite and transition. Rust not recommending Viggo do it since I'm pregnant alarms me. If it has the potential to harm our pup, what can it do to me?

As though sensing my worry, Viggo squeezes my thigh.

"Maya, that's why I hesitated to claim you the first night we met. I won't sugarcoat the enormity of the transition—"

"But Tag bit me, and I'm fine."

My head jerks in Wren's direction. Until now, she remained silent. Her eyes shine with a strength I never saw before. She rises.

"I'm going to shift and show you. Come with me," she says as she extends her hand.

I eye it warily, then remember, this is my best friend. She will never lie to me. Perhaps an omission, but that's okay, given the circumstances. I place my hand in hers.

We go into another bedroom where she strips naked and tells me not to be frightened. She closes her eyes and holds her arms out to the side, palms facing forward. Her body transforms amidst crackling and a flash. A mahogany brown wolf stands on all fours in front of me. Shocked, I gasp and cover my mouth.

Not even in my dream of the red wolf or today have I seen a shift. The impossible is very much real.

Wren shakes her wolf body and sits on her haunches. The same mink brown eyes of her human form stare at me. They flash gold with the presence of her wolf. She's majestic.

I step forward with my hand outstretched. She lowers to her belly, and I kneel beside her large body. Her wolf is not as massive as the guys. But still bigger than a regular one. Her fur is dense beneath my palm. It slides from her head along her back. Her feathery tail thumps on the floor.

"Wow, Wren, you're incredible, chica," I breathe as I sit on my heels. "Did it hurt?"

She shakes her head, and a moment later she's back to human Wren. She puts her clothes on and grins as she hugs me.

"See! A piece of cake. And I'll tell you this… After a shift, you'll be super horny, and Viggo will jump your bones! Oh! And the claiming bite is the most erotic thing ever!"

We giggle as we head to the living room.

The guys turn to watch us walk in. Viggo opens his arms, and I trot over. He pulls me onto his lap and kisses my cheek as his hands cup my belly.

"All good? Not scared?"

"Amazing!"

Everyone laughs.

Then Jagger speaks.

"So, Maya, do you wish to become one with us, allow Viggo to claim and mate with you, accept the transition into a she-wolf?"

Viggo tenses beneath me. I turn from Jagger to him. My eyes scan his face.

"Is that what you want, Viggo?"

"With all my heart. You are my fated mate, Maya. I will never want another female. We belong together as the gods intended. You are already mine."

I take a deep breath before I answer.

His mobile vibrates, dings, and rings beneath my butt. He frowns and slips his hand in his pocket. His scowl deepens as he listens to the person on the line. He ends the call and shifts me to sit on one leg. His fingers fly across the screen.

"What is it?" I ask as nerves creep up my spine.

He growls.

"The fucker who took a photo of you outside of the OB-GYN's office sold it to the media. It's splashed across the Internet."

He turns the mobile around.

Maya Alejandra Perez Garcia Fiancée to Emerico Tonio Santana Rodriguez Pregnant!

Proud Papá Emerico Tonio Santana Rodriguez

Baby Makes 3 for Maya Alejandra Perez Garcia & Emerico Tonio Santana Rodriguez

Is It A Shotgun Wedding for Maya Alejandra Perez Garcia?

"No!!!"

I jump from Viggo's lap and race to the library for my backpack. He runs behind me, calling my name. I snatch the mobile from the inner pocket and turn it on. Immediately, it chimes with alerts.

I sink to the sofa as my father's voice thunders over the speaker. It's the first of many voicemails and text messages, not only from him, but from my mother, brothers, and Emerico.

Viggo growls and pulls me onto his lap as he takes the mobile from me.

"Enough! Do not listen to their bullshit, Maya."

"Oh, honey! They're cruel and selfish!"

I glance up to find Wren and the others crowded around us. Scowls darken their faces. Their eyes flash with their wolves.

"This wasn't how I wanted them to find out. I was going to tell them today," I wail as tears pour down my cheeks.

Viggo holds me tighter and rocks as his rumble begins. Wren sits beside us and pats my back as she murmurs words of support. Their comfort helps the pain slicing through my heart. But does nothing to prevent me from facing my family and Emerico.

Viggo

"Who the hell are you?"

"Are you pregnant, Maya?

"Is this the bastard who knocked you up, *fiancée?*"

It takes every ounce of control for me to wrangle my wolf. Yelling at me is one thing. But shouting at Maya makes him feral. And me. My arm tightens around her waist as we stand in the doorway of her parents' living room.

Maya insisted she speak with her family right away. She changed into a dress and heels Wren selected along with the other items I asked her to buy for Maya while we went to the park. Tag agreed it was better to let Wren stay busy shopping than to sit in the hotel. I expected Maya to wear them for our return trip to Miami, not to speak to her incensed family.

But here we are.

Jagger and Tag rode with us. They wait in the SUV for any word from me to come up to the apartment. Sage used her teleportation magick to reach the hotel. While we're gone, Rust will go with her so she can erase the doctors' minds of the hormone levels and their and my surveillance guys' files. Dylan remains with Wren while she supervises maids to pack our things. They have our back.

Just as I have Maya's back now. I give her a squeeze beforc I address her family.

"If you want to speak to Maya, you better do it with respect. I will tolerate no one hurting her, including you. Do you understand?"

Five pairs of stunned eyes stare at me.

"How dare you come into my home and—"

"I'll cut this short. Maya is pregnant with my baby. She will return to Miami with me where we will marry. I will care for, protect, and love my family with a fierceness you cannot imagine. If you wish to be a part of her and our baby's lives, choose your next words very carefully."

Her father splutters while her mother gasps and clutches her pearls.

Her brothers stare—one with vehemence and the other assesses me.

The fucker's face flames red. He stalks forward, pointing his finger.

My lip curls as my wolf snarls at the threat.

He hesitates.

"Last. Chance."

I growl, skin itching as my wolf claws beneath its surface.

"The engagement is off," the fucker says as he glares between Maya and me, then he turns to her father. "As is the merger."

He storms past us. Fortunately, he has the sense to not bump into me, only to cast a last glare. I narrow my eyes in return. The front door slams shut. Maya jumps with a soft cry.

I cup her face, tilting it up to mine.

"It's okay, my love. We'll leave once you have your say."

She nods as her eyes close briefly. When she reopens them, resolve glistens in their depths.

"*Papá, Mamá.*"

They face her with displeased expressions.

I hear her swallow and squeeze her waist to encourage her. She nods.

"I only learned I was pregnant yesterday afternoon

when that photo was taken. It was not my intention for you to find out through the media. I planned to tell you today—"

"You disappoint me gravely."

"How could you have done this knowing you were to marry Emerico after your twenty-fifth birthday?"

"You made a fool of our family and ruined a profitable merger for our company!"

Before I can respond to her father, mother, and brother, the one who watched me intently whirls on them and shouts.

"Stop! Do you hear yourselves? You. You. You. All your concern is not for Maya and how she must feel with a surprise pregnancy. No! You focus on yourselves. Not to mention it's archaic to arrange a marriage, anyway."

He strides towards us and opens his arms.

"*Hermana*, are you okay?" He asks his sister as she nods and falls into his embrace with a sob. He holds her as they exchange words too low for even my hearing. When they part, she smiles softly. He extends his hand to me. "I'm Patricio, Maya's second oldest brother."

"Viggo Larson," I respond as I shake his hand. "Thank you for caring about your sister. I understand it wasn't expected. But no one may question her. No. One."

I say the last words as I glare at her parents and older brother. Then I turn to Maya.

"Did you wish to say anymore, my love?"

"Yes," she replies and faces her parents. "I never meant to disappoint you. I resigned myself to a life not of my choosing and returned to Caracas willingly. However, I take back my life and will return to Miami, as Viggo said. Should you wish to reconcile, I am open to it. I will always love you. Farewell."

She nods at them and hugs Patricio before she takes my hand. I eye each of them and nod at Patricio. He nods in return.

"I will always love and support you, Maya. Let me know when I can visit. I want to be present for the baby's birth and your wedding. And Viggo, you better do right by my sister. Or you will have to answer to me."

"I would expect no less from a brother who loves his sister."

Maya nods as tears shine in her eyes.

I squeeze her hand and lead her from the living room. Once inside the elevator, she falls into my arms. I scoop her up and rock her as my rumble fills the elevator. I stride through the lobby, ignoring the questioning glances of other residents.

Jagger hops from the passenger seat of the SUV and opens the rear door. I slide in, cradling Maya to my chest. He closes the door and returns to his seat. He glances over his shoulder at me. I nod.

"To the hotel and then the airport. Rest easy, Maya. We'll be home in no time."

CHAPTER 12

"I'VE ALWAYS BEEN curious about Moon Island since I moved to Miami. When Wren told me she and Tag have a place here, I couldn't wait to visit. But she always had an excuse. Now, I realize why…"

Wren giggles as her best friend turns from the helicopter's window to arch an elegant eyebrow.

"Oh, Maya! You know I tell you everything. I just couldn't say a word about the island."

Maya smiles, the first since we left Caracas. She remained quiet when we returned to the hotel, then slept in the bedroom aboard the jet. I held her close, hoping the rumbling would offer comfort. Now, I lift her hand to my lips and kiss the knuckles.

"I will fulfill your curiosity. Tomorrow, I'll give you a tour after Jagger and Sage introduce you to the members of our pack who live on the island. The rest live near or at our camp in the Everglades."

"Once you're on the island, you'll see its true splendor. To protect us from prying eyes—or the curious—I cloak the island with a spell. Upon looking at Moon Island, it resembles the surrounding Venetian Islands, Hibiscus or Palm Islands with mansions and docks along the water and interior with more homes and a park. People move about. However, it's an illusion. No one sees us. We're free to roam about in wolf form…"

As Sage talks, I watch Maya's face. Still adjusting to our Luna being a powerful witch and turned she-wolf, Maya listens intently. Her topaz eyes widen in surprise.

"Wow, who knew! All this time, I thought I saw real people as I zipped by on a Jet Ski. It's so real. I'd never think otherwise."

Sage wiggles her fingers and winks as she says, "Doing my best to keep our pack safe."

Jagger strokes her back as he murmurs in her ear, "Thank you, baby."

Her grin widens as they stare at one another.

Before I fell hard for Maya, I would have joked about their lovey-dovey behavior. Now, I squeeze Maya's hand. My heart swells when she smiles at me and leans her head on my shoulder.

Moments later, the helicopter lands on the island. Golf carts await us. We exchange goodnights and drive to our homes. I'm excited to see Maya's reaction to ours. Along the way, I point out the others' residences. She's impressed. But when we pull into our driveway, she claps her hands and bounces on her seat.

"Ooh! Is this your house?"

I shake my head, and she sits back, peering over her shoulder to the main road.

"It's not my house. This is our home."

I grin as I jump from the golf cart and jog around the front to her side. I scoop her from the seat. She throws her head back and squeals with glee. I carry her over the threshold of the oversized glass door. Her head turns to the accordion glass walls. The lights of South Beach fill the night sky on the other side of Biscayne Bay. The moon reflects on its inky black surface. How apropos where we met and the symbol long associated with wolves stretch out before us. I take it as a positive sign from the gods and grin.

"Welcome home, my love."

She cups my cheek, pulling our faces together for a kiss.

"It feels good to be here. To be with you," she whispers against my lips. "You don't know how much I missed you. I was so scared. And now it's the three of us."

My heart clenches at the sadness in her voice. I can't imagine how she must feel after her family's reaction. Thankfully, Patricio has more sense than the rest of them combined. But I'll make it up to her.

"I missed you so much, Maya. We're together now. And

it's not just us. You'll join the Miami Wolves Pack fully once I issue the claiming bite and you transition—"

I trail off as she shakes her head and averts her eyes. Her arms loosen from around my neck. Hands press against my chest as she tries to stand. My heart stutters beneath her palms.

"What? What's the matter?" I ask, not really wanting to hear her response. Instinct tells me I won't like it. At. All.

"Viggo, let me down. We need to finish the conversation we had at the hotel before your mobile blew up about the photo."

Instead of responding, I stride across the floor and up the stairs. Inside the primary bedroom suite, I sit on the bed. Maya squirms.

"Viggo! I can't believe you take me to your bedroom when I want to talk seriously."

"I've never lived here. There's only basic furniture I ordered for your arrival until you make this into our home. Tell me what's wrong."

She wriggles on my lap, but I tighten my grip.

"I can't sit on the bed?"

"No. Tell me."

She sighs and runs her fingers through her long hair. It cascades down her back, brushing my fingers as they grip her hip. Her gaze focuses on the headboard. Then she speaks.

"Jagger asked if I wish to become one with your pack, allow you to claim and mate with me, accept the transition into a she-wolf. I asked what you want because I'm unsure.

We"—she gestures between us—"don't know one another. One night and equal longing doesn't equate to us knowing one another enough for such a major commitment, especially me becoming a wolf shifter and losing my humanity…"

My grip tightens as my heart races. I thought we were of like mind, even more so after I explained fated mates. Apparently, not. I remain silent. Let her divulge all obstacles. Then I'll plan my strategy. Maya will be mine regardless.

"I wasn't lying when I told my parents I would return to Miami, as you said. However, I didn't affirm the rest. There's no doubt I'm attracted to you. The pull is strong, and I truly missed you. But I need to know you better before I commit to marriage or a mate bonding ceremony. And the claiming bite to transition… At this point, I don't see it happening. Yes, it's incredible how well Wren adjusted to it. But I need more time. My pregnancy delaying the possibility of transition is a sign."

She pauses and gestures around us.

"You want me to stay here and make it our home. Well, my interest in Moon Island and this being a clean slate are more signs. Between now and the birth of our baby-pup, we have over seven months to build our relationship."

She cups my face and stares into my soul.

"Believe me. I want us to be a couple, a family. To have the love and support of your pack. However, I'm still undecided about the transition. That's a hell of a big ask. Give me time. Let's not rush. I hope you understand."

With a sigh, she presses her forehead to mine.

"Okay?"

Thoughts run through my head as my heart pounds in my chest.

Even apart, I've grown attached to Maya. Awaking to her face on her pillow beside me and on the nightstand. Following her activities through past social media posts and her time in Caracas via bloggers, media outlets, and detailed updates from the surveillance team. Plus, the extensive background check provides more about her life. I have a hell of a lot more knowledge of her than she knows of me.

Her wish to learn about me better makes sense.

I'll give her that. But not claiming her as my fated mate? To not bear my mark? Not prove she's mine for all males to see? Out of the question now that she carries my pup.

Over a month without her, followed by news of her pregnancy, and coupled with Wren's positive recovery, lessens my fear of losing Maya during the transition. In my heart, I do not believe the gods would be so cruel as to give me my fated mate, then take her from me.

If I must defy Jagger—my brother and Alpha—to issue the claiming bite against her will, so be it.

～

Maya

. . .

AT VIGGO'S SILENCE, I lean back to scan his face for a reaction to my decision.

His eyes flash silver.

Now knowing he's a wolf shifter, I see the eyes of the red beast within him. My heartbeat ticks up. But I remind myself to relax. I doubt Viggo will ever harm me.

The appearance of his wolf means his emotions run high. Whether it's with anger, as with the bear, with passion while we have sex, or with hurt from my words. I don't want him upset with me. But I won't leave one controlling situation for another. He must understand I get to make decisions in my life.

I wait for him to answer.

Viggo blinks, and the wolf retreats. A fierce determination replaces it. He nods.

"I guarantee after you give birth to my pup, you will bear my mark and join me beneath the mate bonding ceremony bower."

My mouth drops. No. He. Didn't.

He cocks an eyebrow. His finger lifts to my chin and presses up closing my mouth.

I growl.

My eyes widen as my hands clap over my mouth.

What the hell???

Viggo throws his head back and barks with laughter. When he lowers his gaze, it shines with the beast.

"You see, my fated mate, your body knows what it is despite your protests. You carry my pup—a wolf shifter— in your belly. Your genetic makeup blends."

He rises and carries me to a walk-in closet and sets me on the island. He kisses the tip of my nose. His smug chuckle makes me want to growl again. But I hold it back. With a wink, he waves his hand at a wall where all kinds of clothing hang. Then strides to the wall of drawers.

"Signy—you know, my younger sister—shopped for you. I asked her to get some items to carry you over until you went for yourself. As you can see, she filled your entire closet," he says, as he riffles through a drawer. "I said no underwear. She called me a caveman and did as she pleased. Ah… this I like."

He lifts a pale pink silk negligee with cream lace bra cups and a matching robe.

"How about you shower and change into this while I cook dinner?"

He lays the pieces on the island and stands me on my feet. His hands squeeze my hips as he bends his knees to bring our eyes on level. I quirk my lips to the side. He grins devilishly.

"Oh, my little Maya, don't bother to fight it. You know you're mine, and I will make it so. Be a good girl and meet me in the kitchen. I promise your mouth will water for more than my cock."

He turns me towards the door that must connect to the bathroom and spanks my butt. I yelp in surprise as I cover it with both hands. He smirks at my glare, then strides from the closet. I shake my head and let the growl I held back tumble past my lips.

"I heard that, my little wolf!"

"Fuck you, Viggo!"

"Oh, you will…"

I can't help the smile that lifts the corners of my mouth as I continue into the bathroom. I know it should irritate me he sort of disregarded my decision. But the delicious thrum in my pussy from the spank and his parting words overrule.

The smile widens when I spot my favorite toiletries on one vanity. Signy must have spoken to Wren. How thoughtful! I must call her with my thanks.

Not long after, the tantalizing aroma of steak wafts through the air as I enter the kitchen. Indeed, my mouth waters. However, it's not just the food that flares hunger inside my core.

Viggo stands at an impressive stove. Bare chested, his lats and triceps flex as he stirs a saucepan. Fiery copper red hair pulled up in a bun reveals what he calls pack tattoos on the buzzed sides of his head. Black low-slung joggers dip beneath the v cuts at his narrow waist. My eyes track down the long, muscular legs to his toes. My core clenches for the sexy as sin Viking wolf shifter.

"See something you want, Maya?"

I swallow, then quip, "I thought a caveman would prefer his woman pregnant and barefoot in the kitchen, not the other way around."

His hand stills. Slowly, he pivots. His eyes sweep over me from head to toe. The heat in his eyes hardens my nipples. I shift on my feet to ease the ache in my pussy. A smirk tilts his full lips.

"So, you admit you're my woman?"

Before I can respond, he continues, "Good girl."

He leans a hip against the cabinet as he folds his arms over a firm chest. The paw prints move over his pecs. Biceps flex. He cocks his head as his tongue moistens his lips.

"You'll be delighted to learn I enjoy cooking and, as everyone tells me, the food is damn good. So, you will never have to be in the kitchen other than to watch me create dishes to delight you."

He pushes off the cabinet and prowls towards me. His eyes linger on my belly. He crouches before me and places his hands on each side. His lips press to the center before he peers up at me through the thick red fringe of eyelashes a woman would cry for. His eyes flash.

"But I want you pregnant as often as the gods grant us. My son will be the first."

Viggo kisses my belly again and rises with the effortless grace of a predator. His fingertips stroke the sides as his lust-filled eyes train on mine.

I blink to break his carnal spell.

"And how do you know the baby-pup is a boy?"

A smirk full of secrets lifts his lips.

"Instinct. Now, come sit so I can feed you and my pup," he says as he swings me in his arms and carries me to a corner banquette. "Get ready for me to rock your world. Tonight is only the beginning of my Woo Maya Plan."

He growls the last part in my ear as he places me on the leather bench. He sniffs, and I feel his lips spread in a grin.

"I scent your arousal, my little wolf. No worries, I won't only feed you. But I'll feast from your bountiful body every. Single. Day. And. Night."

My eyes flutter closed on a purr as his lips trail from my ear along my jaw to the pulse in my throat. His teeth nip the area as he issues a possessive growl. I shudder. Head lolls to the side to bear my neck. He rumbles and licks the spot before he rises.

My hooded eyes open to watch him stride to the oven. The thick muscles in his legs bunch beneath the joggers. When he returns with one plate loaded with steak and vegetables, his massive cock tents the soft fabric.

Again, I can't decipher whether the aroma of the food or the vision of the wolf shifter causes me to drool. But I do know the next few months will be long and full of temptation. The question is, will I remain strong or fall prey to the red beast?

iggo

"I CAN'T BELIEVE how much is on the island. I figured it only had mansions. This is a self-contained world for wolf shifters!"

Maya giggles as we ride along in a golf cart for the tour of Moon Island.

We left our home, and I pointed out Tag and Wren's grand Mediterranean Revival style residence, followed by Jagger and Sage's Spanish-style one. Rust and Natalie's modern home sits on the other side, next to Dylan and Sasha's Spanish-style one. Each mansion ranges from eight- to ten-thousand square feet. Homes perfectly sized for loads of pups to run, ours included.

As we passed pack members, they wave. Maya returned

their gestures and smiled at me. I told her they know who she is even though they'll gather at the clubhouse in a few hours for her formal introduction. Not much is missed on the island since word travels fast. So far, no negative comments arouse despite Maya being human.

I didn't expect any. As the pack prince and beloved by all, they'll support me. And if they don't, they'll tell me why. Again, no one will disrespect or hurt Maya—pack included.

We're on the other end of the island after passing through the more dense interior where we run as wolves amongst the pine trees and foliage. Here, a mini town offers options for those who prefer not to leave our protected land. A school for younger members of the pack, restaurant, deli, pizza shop, beauty salon, and barber shop are available. And the hospital where we're headed for Maya's OB-GYN appointment with Natalie.

So, yeah, it's an entire world separate from the human one right at their doorstep, or rather the wrought-iron entry gates.

"It is. Which is another reason I brought you here instead of my Ocean Drive penthouse."

She raises her eyebrows in surprise.

"I used to live there, close to Club Hati. The vibrancy of the neighborhood and the vicinity to the beach makes it a perfect spot. I'd love to see your place."

"I can take you. But the building is for the pack bachelors, and there's no way I'd have you stay around a bunch of horny males. I teased Rust when he only stayed there with Natalie until the completion of their mansion. I thought he was being dramatic. Now, I understand why."

Maya rolls her eyes as she shakes her head.

"Seriously? And you don't think you're a caveman? Good grief, Viggo."

"Never said I wasn't," I respond with a smirk, then chuckle when she shakes her head again. "Here we are."

I hop out of the golf cart and help Maya. She glances around the hospital's all-white modern lobby where a receptionist sits behind a desk.

"Hi, Viggo!" She says as she rises and smiles. "You must be Maya. I'm Janice. Welcome to the Miami Wolves Pack. Natalie waits in her office. Rust is on duty at the emergency room on the mainland."

Maya beams and returns Janice's hug.

"Thank you! It's so kind of you to welcome me since I'm human. I must admit your greeting lessens my nerves about the pack introduction later."

"Mostly, we're an open pack. Some were upset about our Luna being a witch. But they got over it. Jagger does not tolerate the mistreatment of any pack member, no matter their origins. Plus, you're with pup. We treasure the little ones as the continuation of our kind. We can talk another time. I don't want to delay you from your appointment. It's just few come to the hospital since wolf shifters heal on their own generally. So, no one for me to talk to. Which is a good thing! I'll see you at the clubhouse!"

Maya grins as Janice shoos us toward the corridor where Rust and Natalie have offices.

True, it's rare a wolf shifter requires medical help. But accidents can happen that require further help. Rust insists on maintaining a state-of-the-art facility with all the latest equipment, two operating rooms, exam rooms, labs, and several patient rooms. They spared no expense to make it the best care facility for our pack. Departments include urgent care, general medicine, obstetrics, and pediatrics. The most used department being obstetrics. Staff besides receptionists include nurses, aides, and the head of administration.

"Hey, Nat!" I say as we enter her office.

She lifts her head where midnight hair streaked with a snow-white widow's peak falls over her shoulder to her waist. Onyx eyes brighten as she smiles.

"Viggo, Maya! Come in. I'm so excited for you!" She says, walking around her desk. Her belly—rounded with Rust's pup—presses against Maya's as she embraces her and grins at me. "Let's sit and chat before the exam. Do you want water or some juice?"

"A water would be great, thanks," Maya responds while I decline.

Natalie gets the water as we settle on the sofa. She hands Maya a bottle and sits on the chair.

"I'm glad you agreed to me as your OB-GYN. I'm experienced with human and wolf shifter births. My speciality is critical care obstetrics. Plus, with all the tests, particularly blood, performed during pregnancy, we can't allow curious minds to question the results."

Maya places the bottle on the coffee table and nibbles her lower lip. The scent of fear fills the air around her.

Automatically, I rumble as one arm wraps around her shoulders and the other hand rests on her belly. The need to soothe her and my pup kicks in.

She leans into me and places her hand over mine.

"What's the matter?"

"I'm scared since I'm human and you're a wolf shifter," she says, then shifts her worried gaze to Natalie. "Do you think our baby-pup will be okay? Already I'm larger than the photos online, and the doctors were concerned with the levels of my hormones. I want nothing to happen to our baby-pup. I want it healthy like any other."

She whispers the last as her eyes drop to Natalie's belly.

She nods with a reassuring smile and responds, "I understand, Maya. Any pregnancy has risks to the mother and baby or pup. I've spoken with the turned she-wolves about their pregnancies and births. None had complications—"

"But they transitioned before they became pregnant. They were she-wolves at the births. I—I'm human, and Rust says it's not advised I transition at this stage. No one else gave birth as a human. I'm scared."

My heartbeat trips at the anguish in Maya's voice. She has mentioned none of her concerns to me.

Natalie sits beside her and pulls her in for a hug.

"Oh, Maya, I understand and don't blame you. Your situation is unique to our pack. However, I reached out to other pack doctors and midwives. Those with a human female giving birth to a pup connected me with them. Only two, but enough to share their experiences. They confirm similar differences in the test results and a shorter pregnancy of six months instead of nine. Hence the higher hormone levels during earlier weeks. They offered to speak with you in case you need reassurance."

I sigh with as much relief as Maya.

Natalie smiles at us and returns to her chair. We talk more about the information she learned before she examines Maya. Then my pulse quickens when Natalie starts the ultrasound.

On the monitor, a tiny face with distinct features appears, followed by the body where hands and feet show fingers and toes. Natalie grins.

"Would you like to know the gender?"

"Yes!" Maya and I shout in unison, then laugh with Natalie.

She changes the position and hovers.

"A male! Yeah, baby! I knew it!" I whoop as I fist pump the air. I lean over to Maya's ear and murmur, "My instinct is never wrong. Trust your fated mate. We were meant to be together as wolf shifters, my love."

She nods as emotions flit across her face.

"You and your pup are in excellent health, Maya. Enjoy your pregnancy and your mate."

I grin at Natalie's last words. She winks and hands a soft cloth to me to clean the gel from Maya's belly.

"When you're ready, come to my office. We'll schedule

your follow-up visits and answer questions you may have," she says before she leaves the exam room.

I turn to Maya and kiss her lips.

"Feel better, now?"

"Yes, so much. A little boy. No wonder I'm so horny with so much testosterone flowing in my system!"

"Ha! Even better!"

She giggles even as her eyes heat. I kiss the tip of her nose and remind her we meet with the pack after this appointment with no time for hanky-panky. She growls, and I chuckle at my little wolf.

Maya

"Greetings Miami Wolves Pack! I sense your excitement about our newest arrival. Your Luna and I are pleased to introduce you to Maya Alejandra Perez Garcia!"

My heart races as I stand on the raised platform and face the pack at the clubhouse.

The two-story structure accommodates their meeting space, recreation rooms, and a grill that serves burgers, fries, shakes, and other backyard-style food. The meeting space fits the large pack, set up with tiered seating and two aisles that lead to the raised platform.

Murmurs arise. Members shift in their seats to get a

better view of the human who sits beside Viggo. Jagger raises his hand to call for silence.

"Maya is Wren's best friend and the fated mate of Viggo. She is pregnant with their male pup. At this time, as a human, Viggo cannot issue the claiming bite to initiate their bonding and her transition. However, Maya is off-limits to any male."

Viggo growls and leans forward, fists clenched.

The males lower their gazes in deference to the pack prince.

I sigh in relief since Wren told me males could challenge Viggo for me as we're not bonded despite me carrying his baby-pup. Her revelation further explains his reluctancy for me to stay at his Ocean Drive penthouse. Surrounded by single males could cause complications within the pack. I have no intention of causing any division. I want everyone to accept me.

"Does anyone have questions?"

Jagger gazes around the space. He nods at an older male who rises.

"Yes, Alpha, if I may?" He says, then continues after Jagger nods. "How do we know Maya won't tell other humans about us?"

"Good question, Frode. She swore allegiance to our pack. As a mother to a future pup, Maya's loyalty is to wolf shifters," he responds, then surveys the crowd. "Any other questions?"

A female stands.

"Yes, Alpha, if I may?" She continues at Jagger's nod. "Where will she stay? On Moon Island or elsewhere?"

"Here, in the home she shares with Viggo. Next?"

Soon the questions end. Sage joins Jagger as he motions for me to stand. Viggo rises beside me. He takes my hand and squeezes it as we face the pack.

"Maya, Luna and I vouch for you and welcome you to the Miami Wolves Pack. Your safety and happiness rank as high as any member," he states, then turns to the pack. "The meeting is over. Kindly welcome Maya!"

They clap and approach the platform to introduce themselves. Three older humans transitioned into she-wolves make their way to the front. They offer me reassurances and their phone numbers with plans for dinner in a few days. I thank them, and they move on.

I notice a cluster of she-wolves flick their gazes between Viggo—who never leaves my side—and me. When I catch their eyes, one stares defiantly while others either avert their gaze or smirk. Not one to back down, I match the stare.

Unexpected possessiveness flares in my chest. I excuse myself and stalk towards the group. Viggo calls my name. But I wave him off. Wren appears at my side. The she-wolves watch as I make my way through those waiting to introduce themselves. I ask for a moment and continue on until I stand before the ringleader.

"Is there a problem?"

Her lips twitch into a sneer as she flicks her gaze over me.

"Ask Viggo."

My nostrils flare.

"Really, Bridget?"

I keep my eyes on the she-wolf as Viggo appears in my periphery. He steps between us, blocking her from my view with his larger frame.

"We fucked, as I did with the others. Do not attempt to make Maya believe it was more. Wolf shifters have voracious appetites. Now, my fated mate feeds me well. I have zero interest in anyone else."

He eyes each of the females until they lower their gazes, then takes my hand and pivots. He puts a hand on Wren's back and guides us to the platform.

"Maya, they mean—"

"No need to explain, Viggo. What you did in the past remains there, along with my—"

He growls as his wolf flashes in his narrowed eyes.

After my reaction to those females, I understand. I cup his cheek and reach up on tiptoe to brush my lips across his mouth. He leans down and nips the lower one between his teeth, then growls.

"Mine and only mine. I will hear nothing of any other male."

"Yes, Viggo," I breathe, aroused by his dominance.

His nostrils flare.

"Come, you'll meet the rest of the pack over the next few days. Right now, you have need of me."

He scoops me and nods at those standing in front of us. They laugh and whoop as he carries me from the clubhouse. Jagger and his best friends' guffaws sound loudest. Viggo ignores their teasing, including those who stand outside as he sets me on the golf cart seat and hops in.

His hand massages my thigh as he drives to our home. Once there, he carries me inside and up to the bedroom where he sits me on the bed. Heat rushes through my body as he strips naked. His gorgeous body with a ginormous cock bare before my eyes makes my pussy flutter. In moments, he removes my dress and lingerie. He puts an arm around me and moves on his knees to the middle of the bed. He pivots and lifts me to straddle his face.

I nearly cum from the sound of his growl as his hands grip my hips. The fingers dig into my flesh as he aligns my pussy with his mouth. A moan slips from my parted lips when the tip of his tongue brushes against my heated pussy lips.

My knees widen to spread my thighs, giving him better access. They quiver as he eats me through two orgasms. My cries of pleasure echo around the empty bedroom.

He kisses both inner thighs then slides up to a seated position with his back against the headboard. His flashing eyes stare into my hooded ones as his dick breaches my folds slowly, inch by delicious inch. Fully seated, my ass rests on his thighs and my fingernails dig into his shoulders. He withdraws just as agonizingly slow. One thrust of his hips, and I'm impaled on his incredible girth. The bulbous tip grazes my G-spot, then press against my womb.

"Aaaahhhh, baby…"

"Fuck yes… So tight, Maya… All mine!"

Once my core adjusts to his size, Viggo's grip on my hips tightens. He lifts me to his tip, then flexes his muscular thighs to snap up and bring me down at the same time.

Shooting stars dance before my closed eyelids as I grip his shoulders to brace myself. So fucking good…

He sets a controlled tempo of slow and deep stokes. His flashing eyes never leave mine after he commands me to open them and to not look away. His hooded gaze burns with passion.

I'm mesmerized.

He continues his thrusts but refuses my cries for release. His commands of *not yet* set my thighs aquiver and my breath to come in pants.

Viggo bands his arms around my waist and hoists me into the air with ease to settle me onto my back. His knees brace on the mattress. His mussed hair falls into his eyes as he places his hands on either side of my head to loom over me.

Did I say sexy AF, or what?

His hips go berserk as he pistons in and out of my greedy little pussy, my thighs tight around his hips. Squelching joins his grunts and my moans. He rides me like a thoroughbred stallion, taking his mare in heat.

My fingernails dig into his biceps as I hold on for dear life.

"Cum… for… me… NOW!" He demands.

The pent-up orgasm rips through me from the top of my head and up from the tips of my toes. My body arcs off the bed as I throw my head back, my mouth open wide in a silent scream. The muscles of my pussy spasm. My juices gush as Viggo tweaks my engorged clit.

Another orgasm followed by another has my mind floating in erotic bliss. The sensation of his dick expanding, then jerking as his hot seed spurts in copious amounts to paint my pussy walls and to fill my womb sends another orgasm through me. It's enough to put another baby-pup inside of me.

A carnal roar rips from his mouth as he yells through his climax to the ceiling.

The air is rich with the scent of our arousal and the mingling of our perfume and cologne with our natural musk. I inhale deeply and close my eyes to savor this moment.

Still hard within me, Viggo lowers his head to my heaving chest. We remain locked in our embrace until our breathing returns to normal.

I brush my fingers through his damp hair, wanting skin-on-skin contact beyond the intimacy of our groins.

He lifts his sated gaze to mine.

"Only you, Maya. No one since, and no one after. I am yours and you are mine," he declares as he holds my chin in his fingers. "I will allow no one to hurt you. Only I will give you pain and know that pleasure will always follow."

I nod as he caresses my lips with the pad of his thumb.

"I love you, Maya."

With a contented sigh, I nuzzle against his neck. Viggo Larson is mine. All. Mine.

*M*aya

"WREN, I still cannot believe you're pregnant with triplets, and we'll give birth around the same time! Talk about besties! Our baby-pups will grow up together. Your little girl will have three brothers instead of two to watch over her!"

I clap my hands as we walk into the Bal Harbour Shops. Viggo and Tag follow behind us. Sage suggested we get clothing for the baby-pups from some stores she and Sasha bought items for their pups. We called ahead and made appointments with personal shoppers to help us with our selections.

Over the past three weeks, I've adjusted well to being pregnant and knowing about the paranormal world. The nausea subsided while my hunger and energy increased, not to mention my sex drive being over the top. Viggo loves it all since he can cook tantalizing dishes for me and do his best to keep up with my stamina. I'm well fed and bred!

Each evening, he shifts into his wolf for our stroll before dinner. He says it's his favorite way to unwind after the office. I love our strolls since we bond while he's a wolf getting me acclimated to the whole wolf shifter side of him.

Pack members wave or stop and chat with me if they're in human form. Wolves keep their distance since Viggo's wolf doesn't want any others near me. The first time one approached, he jumped in front of me, hackles raised, and snarled. They dropped to their backs and bared their necks and bellies in submission. Word spread, and they know better than to come near me.

And no other she-wolves treat me poorly since Sage held a session for the female members of the pack. The Luna reminded everyone to respect each other. She further stressed once a pair mates, former lovers should not refer to their trysts. Some females mentioned instances Sage addressed to ease their minds. The she-wolves who stared at me apologized, and we moved on. I admire Sage's leadership and respect her as the Luna and a friend.

I consider her, Natalie, and Sasha as close friends. We bonded quickly after a Girls' Night In at Sasha's home. She sent Dylan to Jagger and Sage's home to hang out with the guys. We cooked dinner and binge-watched *Vikings:*

Valhalla on Netflix. We agree our guys are sexier than those in the series, and they're some hotties! Later that night, I told Viggo the Norwegian prince turned me on. He growled and showed me why no one compares to the Miami prince.

As promised, the turned she-wolves invited us to dinner with their mates. Wren and Tag joined us. As we ate, each one told her story. They're fated mates—like Viggo insists we are. Prior to meeting their male wolf shifters, they were unaware of the paranormal world and the various beings. The males approached them after detecting their unique scents. They pursued the women without mentioning they could shift into wolves.

Two of the women fell in love with their fated mates right away. The third rejected hers initially. All admitted they felt the attraction and later learned it's the mate bond. What changed the third she-wolf's mind was the persistence of the male. As Viggo does with me, he refused to give up or let her deny him.

Not until the women committed to the relationships did the males reveal their true natures. Their initial reactions were disbelief, fear, and anger. Fortunately for the males, their love proved strong. In time, the women accepted them and decided to be one with them in all ways. The males claimed them.

As with born she-wolves, the humans felt pain and pleasure in the bite. Their cheeks reddened as they described their experiences. The males sat back with smug expressions. Viggo caressed my thigh beneath the table. Aroused by their words, I barely contained a moan.

But their descriptions of the transition brought my attention back from carnal thoughts. After the bite, they felt dazed and slipped in and out of sleep over a course of three to four days. They could only recall the males' constant presence as they fed them soft foods and liquids. In time, they awoke revitalized, more robust than before.

Their wolves appeared on the fringes of their beings. The males taught the new she-wolves how to connect with their other half through their minds and to call them forward to shift. The women described it as their bodies painlessly realigning to the shape of their wolves in moments. They remain in full control of their bodies and their minds. The world appears more vibrant.

They laughed at the increase in their sexual appetites. I giggled, thinking if mine grows anymore, I'll never get out of bed and Viggo would never get to the office. He squeezed my leg knowingly. My cheeks flushed crimson.

Unlike the others, one woman transitioned partially. However, she lives longer with better health. The pack treats her just as they do with the other turned she-wolves.

They completed the mate bonding ceremony—the wolf shifter's version of a wedding ceremony—after their transition. Their eyes grew dreamy as they recalled their special days. Each of them gave birth to a healthy pup. I nodded, remembering Natalie confirmed the human females from the other packs birthed pups in human form too.

Overall, they love their lives with their fated mates, family, and the pack. The women assured me pack life differs little from human families. However, wolves remain loyal and dedicated to the wellbeing of all pack members. The thought of my family's silence other than Patricio and his weekly FaceTime calls made me sad. Viggo rumbled in his chest and put his arm around my shoulders to tuck me against his side.

The women ended with their admiration of the Alpha and Luna since they're fair and loved by all.

Grateful they lessened my nerves, I thanked them. Their positive experiences encouraged me to consider Viggo claiming me fully. But first, I must give birth to our baby-pup.

Along with decorating our new home, we selected the suite closest to ours as the nursery. It comprises a bedroom, playroom, and bathroom. The color palette of greens, blues, and tans makes it a calming space. Bleached wood furniture, hand-painted tiles, and boat accessories keep with the nautical theme. Now, we need clothes for our little one.

Wren smiles brilliantly as she places a hand on her babies bump. Dressed in a silk wrap dress that clings to her BBW figure, she radiates happiness. I'm so proud to see her not only transform into a she-wolf but into a confident female no longer doubtful because of her horrible ex-fiancé. Tag loves and appreciates her, as any smart male should.

"I know, right? I wasn't so surprised when Natalie

confirmed I was pregnant. But when she told me one pup was three, I fainted on the exam table! Naturally, Tag is overjoyed," she says as she glances back at him with a loving smile. "Natalie, me, and now you are pregnant. Sage says the pack shares our excitement."

"Five births within weeks of each other. Incredible. I can't wait to hold our little one."

Wren links arms with me and nods.

"Who would have expected we would be pregnant now, anyway? Funny how fate works," she says, then glances up at me. "As you always tell me, everything happens for a reason, Maya. Trust in it. Viggo truly loves you. He'll suffer wolf madness if you deny your bond. Don't worry. You'll be fine."

I nod since the desire to be one with him increases every day. But I still have time to choose whether I accept his claiming bite and transition or live amongst the pack as his human lover. No need to rush my decision.

We reach the first of three boutiques for children's clothes. Wren and I ooh and aah over the window display with tiny hand-knit onesies, caps, and blankets. Viggo stands beside me and wraps an arm around my waist, drawing me into his side. I place a hand on my baby bump as I lean into him with a contented sigh.

"It still amazes me you're carrying my pup inside of you. Soon I'll hold both of you in my arms," he murmurs as he stares at my reflection in the display window. "I love you both so much, Maya."

My heart clenches. It's times like these my body longs

for his bite. To be his forever. I turn into him, wrapping my arms around his waist as I bury my face in his powerful chest. I inhale his cologne mixed with his natural scent, wanting to imprint it on my mind.

He rubs my back and rumbles, making the world fall away. We're in our own bubble of bliss. One I never wish to leave.

～

Viggo

As I HOLD Maya in my arms, I sense the warring in her mind, as I have recently. I can sense her struggle with the transition. Prior to dinner with the turned she-wolves, Maya was more resolved to not transition instead wanting her humanity. Their experiences combined with that of her best friend cause confliction for Maya.

I also add in to the mix my wooing of her. The more time she spends with me in wolf form, the more comfortable she becomes. Especially when Wren and Tag as wolves join us for walks. It was his idea to help sway her.

Then there's her time on Moon Island interacting with the pack. Movie night in the clubhouse, getting her nails done at the salon, going for pizza all immerse her in our everyday lives. They show we're no different from humans if she sets aside the wolf part.

However, if she denies me after she gives birth to my

son, I will take it back to the Viking days and claim her. Jagger's wrath be damned. I'll take my fated mate and pup to another pack or go rogue like Dylan. Maya is mine, and no one or nothing will stop me from completing our bond.

I loosen my hold around her and lift her chin with my index finger. Her eyes shine with love in a gorgeous face aglow with impending motherhood. I brush the pad of my thumb over her lips.

"Let's get my pup ready."

The smile that spreads across her face could make the gods sing.

"Yes, Viggo. And I love you too."

I suck in a breath, and she kisses my thumb. I cover her mouth with mine for a passionate kiss.

"Oh, get a room or get inside the store."

We break apart, laughing at Tag's wry remark. Mr. Grumpy shakes his head and ushers Wren inside. We follow laughing.

"Welcome to Bonpoint!"

A salesperson greets us as the door closes. She glances between Maya and Wren's rounded bellies. I can't believe Tag put three pups inside of her. I'll have to up my game.

"Thank you," Maya and Wren say in unison, then giggle.

"We have appointments," Maya adds.

The salesperson nods and confirms their names. She introduces herself as the shopper for Wren and calls to a female folding a sweater. She walks over and introduces herself as Maya's shopper. We pair off and sit on sofas to discuss our needs. When the shopper asks about our budget, Maya hands her the AMEX Centurion Card and grins at me.

One of the first things I did following Maya's arrival on Moon Island was to arrange the Black Card along with bank accounts for her. I scheduled monthly fund transfers and automatic payments to cover her expenses. Maya will never worry about the cost of a damn thing. She can buy whatever the hell she wants. Her parents can go kick rocks since they cut her off. Fuckers.

Her eyes widened in surprise when her card and her bank details arrived. She didn't realize I was a multibillionaire on my own, aside from my family's wealth. I invest wisely.

I grin back at her as the shopper pockets Maya's card.

We spend the next few hours in two stores before we break for lunch. The girls decide only Italian food will do. They lead the way to Carpaccio. The hostesses do a double take when they glance up from the podium. Their eyes flick between Tag and me with interest. We place our arms around Wren and Maya. Growls vibrate in their chests. The hostesses blink.

"A table on the patio for four."

They nod, and one hurries to gather the menus before she leads us to the sun-drenched patio. Tag and I help the girls into their chairs, then sit. The hostess hands the menus to us, careful to keep her gaze down as Maya and Wren glare at her flushed face. She mutters an *enjoy your lunch* before she scampers away. If she had a tail, she would tuck it between her legs.

Tag and I glance at each other and laugh.

"Not funny," Wren snarls as her wolf flashes in her eyes. The petite beauty did not appreciate the other females ogling her mate. Nor did Maya, who growls in agreement.

I press a kiss to her check as my hand kneads her thigh beneath the table.

"Only you, my love. Only you," I murmur against the delicate shell of her ear, then trail kisses along the column of her neck. A nip to the juncture of her shoulder makes her yelp. I lap the spot and kiss it. A reminder of the claiming bite I will issue.

When I sit back and smirk, her hooded eyes stare at me glistening like the precious stone their color resembles. If she continues to react this way, she'll give in to me without me forcing the bond. Either way, it will happen.

A server appears. He rattles off the day's specials and takes our drink orders. When he steps away, Maya and Wren chatter about the dishes they crave. In the end, they decide on a smorgasbord with citrusy Riviera salads, Margherita pizza, and paper-thin, succulent beef, tuna, and salmon carpaccio. Their mouths watered for the special of linguine with lobster, shrimp, mussels, and clams in a red tomato sauce. I order it so they can have some. Tag goes for the sirloin steak with green peppercorn, brandy, and cream.

While we eat, talk centers on the items we found so far, what is missing from their lists, getting toys for the nurseries, and all pup things. A goofy grin remains on my face. I glance up to find Tag smirking at me. I shrug, completely busted. What can I say? I'm an excited papa-to-be. He nods in agreement as his gaze slides to Wren. We chime in as needed. But they keep the conversation going until we finish and they're ready for the last store.

When we drive up to Moon Island's entry gates, the security guards wave and gesture to the building where they place deliveries. Tag and I hop out of Maya's new Mercedes-Benz G-Wagen I purchased to replace the one she sold when she left Miami. We load the packages from the stores into the back. With an abundance of bags, Maya and Wren hold some on the back seat. They giggle as we pile the bags on the floor and their laps. Before I shut the door, I zerbert her golden cheek tinged rosy as she laughs. Her topaz eyes sparkle. So beautiful. And all mine.

We drop Tag and Wren off first. I help him carry the bags inside as Wren hugs Maya. The couple wave as we drive off. At our home, I park in the four-car garage and help Maya from the truck. She wraps her arms around my neck and grins.

"What a great day! I'm so happy."

I nuzzle my face in her neck where I will place my mark and breathe in her unique scent. The intoxicating aroma of fragrant frangipani mixed with fresh coconuts and salt carried on a tropical breeze from the Caribbean Sea fills my lungs anew. I say a silent prayer to the gods, thanking them for my fated mate, who I will claim soon. My wolf can barely wait a second longer, and neither can I.

 *iggo*

"So, how are things going with Maya? What did she decide about the transition? Not much time left since she'll give birth in a just over a month."

Jagger asks as we stroll along the interior of Moon Island. Glancing at me, he cocks a white blond eyebrow.

I take a moment to consider.

During the past ten weeks, she's expressed her love for me and happiness we're together with my pup on the way. She hasn't mentioned the transition—neither as a no or a yes. More often, I nip the spot on her neck. She no longer swats at me or wiggles away. This morning, she moaned and tilted her head to the side to give me better access. I increased the pressure of my fangs. She mewled as the scent of her arousal wafted to my nostrils.

Her reaction tempted my wolf. With great effort, I lifted my mouth away from her neck as the serum dripped from my fangs. The warm liquid pooled at her collarbone, and she moaned. My wolf remains on edge despite Maya and me being a couple. His patience wears thin. He wants to claim her fully. Now. As do I.

"She's amenable."

He pauses and faces me. He folds his arms across his chest. Muscles ripple as he cocks his head. Ice blue eyes regard me intently.

"Care to elaborate?"

Not really. But judging by his dominant stance, Jagger speaks as pack Alpha, not as older brother. His concern focuses on Maya, a potential member under his protection. Even from her fated mate, should she not wish to proceed with the bonding.

I run a hand through my hair, tugging on the loose strands. The bite of pain clears my head.

"We're in a good place. She's happy, excited about being a mother, tells me she loves me every day. She made my mansion into our home, blending our styles into a harmonious sanctuary. You know she's into crystals, feng shui, and all."

I glance over his shoulder at movement behind him. An elder couple approaches. They stop to talk. Once they move on, I start to walk.

"You missed a question."

Jagger's statement stops me mid-stride.

Naturally, he didn't forget about the transition.

I turn to face him. He raises an eyebrow.

"She hasn't said no," I say, hedging. Then he growls as his wolf flashes in his eyes. "Fine. She's more responsive when I nip her neck, no longer pushes me away. I expect she'll consent after she gives birth."

He studies my face. Satisfied, he nods.

"Excellent. I expect you to obey my command, Viggo. Do not try me."

"Yes, Alpha," I respond with fingers crossed behind my back. I keep a straight face to prevent him from detecting any deceit.

His eyes narrow and nostrils flare as he scents the air. My eyes remain lowered out of respect. He steps forward, and I brace for impact. His arms raise.

"Good to hear, bro!" He exclaims as he claps me on both shoulders and presses his forehead to mine. "I want you to experience the unfailing love of a fated mate and the joys of fatherhood. Sage has changed my life from a playboy like you to a happy husband."

"Months ago, I would have laughed. But after meeting Maya, that's all I want too."

He squeezes my shoulders and pivots.

"You've matured so much since you joined Larson Enterprises. Every year, you offer new recommendations that prosper and your division reaches—if not surpasses—its revenue goals. You've impressed not only me but our business partners. During many meetings, one will mention you and one of your projects. You've made a name for yourself in the industry. Excellent."

He glances at me and nods.

"Now, with Maya and a pup on the way, you will have more responsibilities. I believe you will be as great a father as you are a businessman. I'm proud of you, Viggo."

My chest swells with pride. At last, the recognition I wanted and more.

"Thank you, Jagger. You don't know how much that means to me, brother."

While we continue our walk, I launch my own list of questions for his advice. After a half an hour of baby prep talk, babymoon, and push present—push present???—suggestions, diaper changing hits or misses, and post-natal intimacy, we shoot the shit. We part at his driveway.

"See you in a few hours."

"Yup, see you at the clubhouse."

I wave and head down the street and onto my driveway. Inside the mansion, I call for Maya. But no answer. I check my mobile, then call hers when I don't see a text message. She went to the salon with the girls to gussy up for the pup shower this afternoon.

"*Ciao, Mi Amor!*"

"*Ciao hermosa.* How's it going? Almost done?"

In the background, Signy giggles about Sasha's joke. Her distinctive Russian accent stands out from the others. Maya giggles before she responds.

"Wonderful! We're almost done. Natalie and Wren sit at

the dryers. We'll leave in a few minutes. How was your walk with Jagger? Sage wants to know if he's home yet."

"Good and yes. I left him at their house a few minutes ago. I won't hold you up. See you in a bit. I love you."

"I love you too. *Besos para usted, Mi Amor.*"

We end the call with the girls teasing her about blowing me kisses. I grin and jog up the stairs to shower. I'd wait for Maya. But I doubt she'd want me to mess up her hair. When I step out of the bathroom with a towel wrapped around my hips, I hear a sound in her walk-in closet. I stride over.

"Hey, babe, you're back already—"

But the words get stuck in my throat. Before me is a dick hardening sight.

My eyes travel over her lush body covered in a black silk bra and thong. Since we skinny-dip, no tan lines mar her flawless golden skin. Long, silky waves cascade to brush her round ass. It gobbles up the thin strip, emphasizing the fullness of each cheek. I lick my lips as my mouth waters.

"*Hola, Amante,*" she purrs.

My hungry gaze lifts to her reflection in the trifold mirror.

Maya glances over her shoulder at me with a lust-filled expression in her eyes. She narrows them seductively when she sees my mouth hanging open and my eyes fixed on her enticing bottom. She shimmies her hips and her voluminous breasts bounce in the silk demi cups.

With a low growl, I loosen the towel to free my dick. I

advance with a predatory gleam in my eyes. With a snap of my wrist, the thong rips. She gasps as it pinches her clit. My cock thumps at her cry. I release the bra hooks and growl as her ample tits slip from the cups. She whines as I knead the heavy mounds and tweak the plump nipples to distended peaks. I bend my body over hers to lower her into a ninety-degree angle, ass high. A hand lowers to cradle her pup bump.

My growl deepens when I line my rapidly hardening shaft with her seam and impale her instantly. Both of us groan in mutual satisfaction as we join as one in absolute carnal rapture.

Since I entered Maya with no preparation—yes, she definitely drives me mad—I spank her ass to give her pussy time to grow accustomed to my girth and length. I move at a slow, rhythmic pace. Her juices coat my cock as her arousal catches up to mine. The feeling of being bare inside of her is indescribable. My cock feels every surface of her pussy walls, including the texture of her G-spot that I brush my tip against each time I re-enter her core. The increased movement of her ass hitting back against my groin pushes my dick deeper within her drenched folds. My tip touches her womb.

Again, my inner caveman surfaces and grunts as I mount Maya and increase my pace, plundering faster and harder, wanting to plant my seed deep into her fertile womb. I adjust my grip, placing one hand on the top of her shoulder to hold Maya in place. The other hand I place under her opposite thigh to lift it, changing the angle to go even deeper. The sounds of our mating reverberate around the room.

I feel her walls tremble, milking up and down my cock as I squeeze her clit with the fingers under her thigh. She tosses her head back and wails my name as she convulses with her orgasm. I lift her off the floor to drive up into her pulsating pussy. Mad in my desire to fuck her raw, I chase the orgasm brewing at the base of my spine.

"Fuck yes, baby... Take it... Take all of it... YES!" I shout, my voice gruff with desire.

My movements become disjointed as I feel Maya cum for the fourth time and my dick swells deep within her sopping wet pussy. I shift to face the wall and brace her against it as I ram into her again and again until I can't hold back any longer. I grip her hips tightly and posses-sively bite the sensitive area where her shoulder meets her neck as my orgasm rips through my body. My cock jerks deep inside of her, erupting with seed that coats her womb. I can't stop thrusting like the feral beast I am claiming its mate until every drop of my jizz spews from my tip.

My knees weaken and I lower us to the floor, pulling a boneless Maya into my lap. My spent dick falls from her pussy that's dripping with our combined essence. I stare at the puddle forming beneath our entwined legs, transfixed by our coupling. She sighs and lays her head against my chest where my heart beats helter-skelter.

"Sorry I messed up your hair."

~

Maya

"SURPRISE!"

I place a hand over my heart as Viggo removes the silk blindfold from over my eyes. I glance around to find Wren and Natalie equally surprised. Their mouths form perfect Os as they clutch Tag and Rust. The pack continues to chant. I glance up at Viggo.

He grins and kisses my cheek.

"Surprise, Hot Mama. The pack wants to celebrate the upcoming births with a pup shower."

A smile replaces the questioning expression on my face. I wrap my arms around his neck and whisper thanks. Keeping a hand on his arm, I face those gathered on the lawn behind the clubhouse. They wave and whoop.

"Thank you! Thank you so much!"

Wren and Natalie echo my sentiments. We move forward to join the pack. They decorated in shades of pink, cream, blues, and grays. Sofas and chairs arranged around six throne-like chairs with tables and chairs covered in white linen fill the space. To the side, rows of tables laden with delicious smelling food make my stomach growl. Still more tables overflow with gifts. Digital photo booths with frames of our names and drawings of wolf pups stand to one side. Stations labeled with various games sit throughout the space. Instead of a baby shower limited to women, they included the guys for a full pack affair. It's a giant party!

Jagger and Sage step forward. The crowd quiets.

"We're excited to have new additions to the Miami Wolves Pack! Today we celebrate the mothers who will give us such precious gifts. Thank you, Natalie, Wren, and Maya."

We thank the Alpha and Luna. Sage embraces us and guides us to mingle with the others. Viggo remains by my side with his hand on my lower back. Just his touch causes tingles to radiate through me. His unexpected, aggressive fucking drove me wild. *Ay Dios mío.*

He must sense my renewed arousal. His hand strokes up my spine to grip the back of my neck. He gives it a squeeze, and my knees wobble. He chuckles and braces my back against his front.

"Easy, greedy girl. I'll ravish you again later."

"Promise?" I ask breathily, then moan as he leans down and nips my neck before sliding his teeth up to my ear.

"Promise," he rasps in a voice thickened with desire.

A shudder runs through me. This male right here...

Wren's squeal pulls me from the lust fog.

I glance over at her where she stands beside a game station. She waves a piece of paper in her hand as she giggles. Tag takes it from her and reads it. He smirks and whispers in her ear. Her cheeks blossom bright red. He chuckles and kisses her cheek.

"Whatever that is, I want some of it."

We laugh at a single she-wolf who fans herself. Another female bobs her head in agreement. A handsome pack bachelor sidles between them and drapes his arms over their shoulders. He flicks his gaze between the two.

"I volunteer myself for whatever pleasures you desire."

One nibbles her lower lip while the other winks. They walk off, heads bent together.

"All righty, then!" Another male says as he guffaws. "We'll have another pup shower in a few months."

"Yes, there's something about mate bonding ceremonies and births. Everyone gets the itch," a she-wolf adds.

Viggo tucks me against his side and moves us along. We chat with others as pack members acting as servers pass through with trays of finger foods and glasses of iced tea. We enjoy the games and take photos before we settle down at the tables for a late lunch.

Afterwards, Sage and Sasha lead us to the throne-like chairs. They hand us gifts to unwrap as the pack watches from the sofas and chairs. Dozens of onesies, hand-crocheted blankets, plush wolves, books, toys, and more pile up on the tables behind us. We'll need a truck to bring the gifts home and a second nursery to put them in.

Everyone is so loving and don't differentiate my baby-pup from Wren and Natalie's pups. My heart swells. Viggo and I exchange several glances. He's as thrilled as I am. His handsome face flushed with joy as he laughs and holds up a wooden train set. The whole affair turns into a fun fete we enjoy for hours.

A sharp cry from Natalie quiets the space. Rust jumps to his feet as she places her hands on her both sides of her belly. She glances up at him and nods. He barks orders to clear the way and to bring a golf cart from the front of the clubhouse. Dylan races to get one. Jagger rushes to Natalie's side and asks Rust how he can help.

In moments, Rust has Natalie in the golf cart and drives to the hospital with Jagger and Sage. Dylan and Sasha hurry for another cart. Viggo and Tag insist Wren and I go home despite our protests, citing the excitement may be too much for us at this stage of our pregnancy. The pack agrees with the overly protective males and offers to deliver the gifts. Viggo scoops me up as Tag does the same with Wren. They carry us to golf carts and take us home.

I wave as they turn into their driveway. Wren crosses her fingers, and I return the gesture with a prayer for Natalie. I place a hand on my baby bump as I wonder what she experiences. Viggo covers my hand with his. I glance at him.

"Don't worry. Natalie will be fine. Rust will deliver his pup as he did for other she-wolves and their little ones before Natalie joined the pack. It'll be your turn soon, baby. And then I will make you mine."

aya

"THESE ONESIES ARE TOO CUTE! Look at the little wolves doing cartwheels!"

Sage giggles as she holds the tiny outfit up.

"I love it!" Wren exclaims. "And get a load of this one with teddy bears!"

We're in my baby-pup's nursery six weeks after the surprise baby shower. It was so much fun to play the games and to open the many presents while we interacted with the pack members.

But the biggest surprise was Natalie giving birth to a healthy male pup. Rust delivered him with no problem, as Viggo said he would. With her advanced healing, Natalie recovered in a few days. However, she took a leave of absence from her OB-GYN duties at the mainland hospital. Thankfully, she confirmed she will handle the deliveries for Wren and me, much to Tag and Viggo's relief. They got all growly at the possibility of Rust covering for Natalie. Cavemen...

Since the shower, I've had the urge to nest. Hence reorganizing the gifts we received along with others delivered in the last few days from the other five major wolf shifter packs. I've even reordered my baby-pup's supplies in his bathroom!

Sasha says it's a natural instinct to use the burst of energy I've gotten to prepare for his arrival. It's no different from mama birds, cats, and other humans—male included.

I drive Viggo nuts with moving his things into an order I think works best. The other morning, while I was in the library reorganizing the books to make room for the first editions of *The Bobbsey Twins* and *Winnie The Pooh*, he came in asking where I put his ties.

He didn't quite understand why I moved them from their drawers to racks behind his suits. I figured he picked a suit, then would move down the row to pick a tie.

Well, no. So, I spent an hour putting them all back.

I roll my eyes at the memory. Then straighten up to glance at the onesies Signy and Wren hold.

"Oh, those came from Garrett Moen, the Alpha of the New York Wolves Pack. A baby boutique in New York—"

A sharp pain in my lower belly and lower back makes me double over with a cry. The pain radiates down my legs, making my knees buckle. I whimper and clutch my belly when I realize I'm falling.

But instead of hitting the floor, two sets of hands hold me up.

"We have you, Maya!" Sasha exclaims.

"Deep breaths, Maya," Sage tells me calmly. "Focus on your breath."

They maneuver me to the glider, and I sit gingerly. The bracelet on my wrist beeps. A second later, my mobile rings.

Viggo.

Concerned he would be at the office when I went into labor, he purchased a monitor to track vitals, particularly for erratic or elevated heart rates that deviate from the norm. Plus, it has a fall detection and a GPS tracker for the location of the wearer. He gave one to Wren and one to me. The app connects to the monitor, then alerts Viggo, Tag, Natalie, Rust, Jagger, and Sage.

Sasha answers my mobile while Sage checks my vitals.

"Maya! What's happening?!" Viggo asks over the speakerphone.

I start to speak, but another cramp hits me and knocks the breath from my lungs. Instead, a pitiful moan spills from my lips as I grimace.

All morning my back bothered me, but I just assumed it was gas from the French onion soup I ate last night. I craved the crouton and broth. It was yummy then, but it repeated on me… So, I ignored the pangs.

Wrong.

"I'm on my way there!" Viggo shouts and disconnects the call.

Sage asks me questions while Sasha answers Natalie's call. They relay my answers to her, and she advises we come to the hospital even though my water hasn't broken. Since we can only guess at my due date, Natalie doesn't want to risk me going into labor at home. She will meet us at the hospital.

Just as they stand me on my feet, Dylan rushes through the nursery room's door. He takes one glimpse at me and scoops me from the glider. He rushes for the door. Sasha grabs my hospital bag. Sage helps Wren. Signy follows.

"Hold on, Maya, I got you!" Viggo says as we hurry down the stairs. "Just breathe like Natalie taught you."

"Yes. Don't worry, just focus!" Sasha adds with a nod. "You and your pup are all good!"

I smile at their words. But the grin gets wiped off my face a moment later when I feel a popping sensation, along with a slow trickle of fluid between my thighs.

OMG!!! Did I just pee on myself???

Embarrassed, I peek at Sasha, then Dylan. She doesn't notice. However, he picks up on my discomfort.

His nostrils flare as he cocks his head to the side. He nods and tells me not to worry.

I glance down at my lap, then at him with wide eyes as we walk through the front door Sasha holds open. I'm wearing a white off the shoulder loose tunic and black leggings. At least the dark color will hide the evidence of my oopsie. Although I'm certain it ruined my silk thong and his sweater.

He nods in understanding and turns to Sasha.

"Babe, before you put Maya on the golf cart's seat, can you place a towel down?" he asks.

She nods, and Dylan's gaze shifts from me to Sage to Wren.

"Did your water break?" She asks softly.

I flush bright red and nod.

"It's okay, Maya. That's good! Your pup is on his way!" She exclaims with a smile so full of happiness my heart flutters with joy.

Then Wren cries out.

We turn to her in unison as Dylan sits me on the seat. She grasps her belly and frowns. Sage says it's Wren's time too. Dylan lifts her into his arms and places her next to me. We huddle together as he gets behind the wheel and Sage, Sasha, and Signy hop in. Soon we arrive at the hospital.

Natalie and two midwives wait for us. As the midwives push us in gurneys down the corridor, she tells us Rust is on his way from the hospital and Viggo and Tag will land at the helipad soon.

They place Wren and me in separate patient rooms. As we part, we stare at each other scared, until Natalie assures us we'll be fine. Sage and Signy go with Wren and Natalie while Sasha stays with me. Dylan excuses himself as his mobile rings. The midwife helps me to change into a clean gown and robe, then makes me as comfortable as possible on the bed.

I settle back and focus on my breathing. *Stay calm, Maya. You can do this!*

"Fuck!!! What the hell did you do to me, Viggo Larson?!?!?!"

I scream at the top of my lungs as I glare at him. Daggers don't even come close to the dangerous weapons of mass destruction I'm throwing in his direction.

He stares back at me wide-eyed with his mouth agape. My Viking warrior is no longer in control. He's in shock.

I've been in active labor for almost seven hours. Seven. Fucking. Contraction-Filled. Hours…

"How much longer, dammit?!?!?!" I screech.

The contractions come faster and last longer now. I want to bear down. A lot of pressure stabs my lower back, worse than before and now in my rectum. I want to push, but the midwife tells me not yet.

After Natalie settled Wren in her room, she prepped me for the first stage of pregnancy, pre-labor. She explained in first-time pregnancies, it can take six to eight hours for my body to be ready for the actual delivery. Once my cervix dilates to ten centimeters, she expected the second stage to be as short as twenty minutes or as long as a few hours.

Hell to the no, no, no! Not another minute, let alone a few fucking hours!

"Let's have the midwife check your cervix. Since the contractions are coming closer together and occur for ninety seconds, you may be ready," Sage suggests as she massages my calves.

Sasha agrees, and Sage steps out. Jagger and Dylan sit in the waiting room.

Since Wren and I are in labor, they split between my room and hers. I haven't had a chance to speak with my bestie, so I don't know how far along she is in labor. I only know hers will be quicker since she's a turned she-wolf.

Right now, I can't think past this pain honestly.

Ay Dios mío.

"Let's have a peek, Maya."

I raise my gaze to see the midwife and Sage walk through the door. She helps me to lean back against the pillows while the midwife peeks under the sheet.

"Well, well, well, your cervix dilated to ten centimeters. I'll get Natalie now," she says with a warm smile and a gentle pat to my knee.

"Oh, thank you, Lord!!!" I cry.

Viggo takes my hand in his and smiles as he says, "Babe, you're doing so well. Soon it'll be over, and we'll have—"

He yowls as I grip his hand with all my strength when an excruciating contraction rocks me to my core.

"Fuuuck!!!" I bellow, followed by a string of curses. I call Viggo every name I can think of and then find some more.

The midwife chuckles as she heads to the door.

"Viggo, would you like me to have a look at your hand?" She asks over her shoulder.

"No, thank you. That's all right," he grunts as he rubs his hand.

Sage rises from the chair and reaches for Viggo's hand.

"It's not the best idea to hold a female's hand when she's

in labor," she laughs as she massages his hand with her fingertips. "Ask your brother and Dylan. I'm sure I broke one or two of Jagger's fingers!"

Viggo groans, "Lesson learned, Sage, thanks."

Natalie enters, and I say a silent prayer.

"Sounds as though you're ready for me, Maya," she says. "Let's have a look."

Viggo growls softly when she takes a seat on the stool at my feet and lifts the sheet. She smiles at him reassuringly before she lowers her head and peers between my legs.

"All right, Maya, we're in the second stage of labor. The time to push is now," she says.

"Thank the good Lord!!!" I cry as another contraction hits me.

"He's crowning. Get ready to push, Maya," Natalie raises her eyes to mine and nods. "All right, now! Push!"

At once, I curse myself for not accepting the epidural when I had the chance. My and my not wanting to put anything unnatural in my body… I feel as though I have a hundred of Viggo's massive hard dicks battering my pussy for hours with no end.

"AAARRGGGHHH!!!" I growl as I bear down.

"Breathe with it, Maya. Breathe," Sage says as she stands to my right, just in my line of sight. "Focus on your breath."

I take a deep inhale in preparation to increase the pressure within my belly and contract my abs. Holding my breath before I let it go as I push our baby-pup out.

"That's it, my love. You're doing well," Viggo murmurs

as he strokes my hair that Sage put into one long braid down my back.

My mind knows it's not his fault. Well, not entirely. But I just can't think straight at a time such as now.

"Shut up, Viggo!!!" I growl as I slap his hand away from me with a kyber crystal-powered super laser stare from the Death Star. It's strong enough to destroy an entire planet. Or a Viking.

Viggo opens his mouth, then thinks better and closes it. He glances at Sage, and she shakes her head, suppressing a giggle.

It's rare one sees the powerful wolf shifter at a loss and not in charge of a situation.

More contractions, more choice words, more killer looks, more pushing, and our baby-pup makes his debut.

Viggo

MY PUP IS BORN!

Holy shit! I'm a father, a Dad, a *Papá*.

"Viggo, you may cut the umbilical cord now."

Natalie's words pull me from my pleasant musings, and I glance at her. She hands a pair of sterile scissors to me with a broad smile and a nod of encouragement.

I shift my gaze to Maya, my fated mate, my love, the mother of my pup. Her topaz eyes—softened by the miracle she achieved—stare back at me from a face flushed red and damp from the exertion of nine hours of labor.

My heart swells and my eyes well with tears. I lean over to kiss her on her lips, then press my forehead to hers as I close my eyes on a silent prayer of thanks to the gods.

"I love you, Hot Mama. Thank you," I murmur huskily as tears slip down my cheeks.

Maya reaches a small hand up to wipe the moisture away. She brings her wet fingertips to her lips, then places them on mine.

"I love you, *Papá*. Thank you, my love," she whispers in a hoarse voice. "Cut the umbilical cord so we can hold our son."

She pats my cheek and sighs, exhausted from the delivery.

With a nod, I turn to Natalie and do the honor. The pediatrician takes my pup off to the side in order to care for him. I split my gaze between her actions and Maya, who's being comforted by Sage. I confirm she's fine, then turn my full attention to our pup.

"How is he?" I ask as I watch possessively over the doctor's shoulder while she tends to him.

She smiles at me and responds, "He's in excellent health! All ten fingers and toes! He weighs 7.8 pounds. An acceptable size for a male newborn. Congratulations, Viggo!"

Relief washes over me. Then anxiety sweeps in when she places our freshly cleaned son in my arms. When I look at her in a panic, she smiles encouragingly.

I glance down at his mottled face. He may be tiny, but the weight of responsibility hits me in that moment. My son, the fruit of my loins. I am his father. His safekeeping ranks as my utmost priority, along with his mother.

"Viggo? What's taking so long? Is he okay?"

Maya's soft voice filled with concern calls me back to the room.

"He's perfect, my love. See for yourself," I respond as I stride over to her and place our pup on her chest.

Her face lights up with such love and joy when she stares at him. Tears stream down her cheeks. Her fingers tentatively touch his soft jet black hair, and his eyes open slowly.

Ice blue eyes and jet black hair. The perfect combination of his parents.

Maya peers up at me and smiles angelically.

"Your baby-pup, my love," she whispers. "He looks like you, like a true Viking. Are you pleased, Viggo?"

I nod, overwhelmed, and I bury my face in her damp hair.

An hour later, a freshly washed Maya holds our pup to her breast as she feeds him for the first time. They're skin-to-skin to help him stay warm as he gets used to being outside of her womb. Natalie explained it's a great way for parents and pup to get to know each other right away. Our pup welcomes our gentle touches, and this closeness can help us bond with him.

I rub his back beneath the blanket, wanting him to recognize his sire, too. My hand is so much larger than his narrow back. I smile and pull my mobile from my pocket to take a video and some photos.

Maya giggles and pats the bed beside her.

"Come, sit, *Papá*," she says, with a twinkle in her hazel eyes.

I smirk when, for a moment, my mind drifts to the fetish. But that's not our thing. Although we'll try anything once...

"Stop it! Viggo..." Maya laughs. "Sit with us before others come in. I'm just sad my family isn't here. We didn't have time to tell Patricio. Hopefully, he can visit soon."

As tears fill her eyes, I cup her cheek. I won't let those fuckers ruin our first family bonding moment. When Maya sleeps, I'll reach out to Patricio to invite him to visit—not on Moon Island, of course. I'll arrange for Maya, our pup, and me to stay at a visitor's apartment in The Larson Tower while he's here.

I turn my mind away from negative thoughts and focus on what truly matters. I have my family of Maya, our pup, and me. Our family unit that fits inside of the Miami Wolves Pack. Now, I know how Jagger and Dylan feel. To have my own is the most incredible sense of responsibility. Mine to care for, mine to protect, mine to love forever.

Mine!!!

"Tell me, did Wren give birth to her triplets?" Maya asks. Her eyes pop in concern for her best friend, even on the heels of her delivery.

I smile before I put my mobile in front of her to hold it

as our pup suckles at her breast. With a few swipes, I load the video Tag sent earlier.

"Here, see for yourself, babe," I say as the screen fills with a grinning Tag angling his mobile to capture Wren, their pups, and himself.

"Hi, bestie! Guess who made their debut?" Wren trills.

Tag moves his mobile closer to their tiny faces. Their little rosebud mouths purse, and they open their eyes to reveal emerald eyes like their sire.

"My sweet pups. Can you believe it?" Tag says in awe.

Wren gazes at him with such love. Then faces the mobile again, and her mink brown eyes shine.

"Now it's your turn to send a video message!" She laughs.

"Yes!" Tag adds as he waves before the video ends.

Their intimacy tugs at my heart. This is what Maya and I have now. I'm beyond ecstatic.

As I put my mobile down, it vibrates with a call. A glance at the screen shows Jagger's name. Maya and I have been so focused on enjoying these first few moments with our pup we hadn't communicated with him, Sage, or the others.

"Hey, bro! We're all good. Give us a minute before you come in to meet your newest pack member!" I exclaim.

Maya laughs as she puts him on her shoulder.

I rub his back to help him burp. The greedy bugger. While Maya fixes her nightgown and robe, I cradle our pup to my chest through the opening of my button-down shirt. He's warm from Maya and smells like a newborn, just as I remember Signy.

"I'm all set, Viggo," Maya says on a yawn.

"You need to rest, babe," I respond and continue when she starts to object. "We'll announce his name, make the video, and take some more photos. Afterwards, everyone leaves. It's important you take care of yourself, *Mamá*."

She grins and nods in agreement.

I place our pup back in her arms, and she nuzzles his hair, inhaling his unique scent. Before I let the others in, I take a moment to stare at my little family.

All mine!

As soon as they walk in, Sage makes a beeline for Maya and our pup. She coos softly as she strokes his chubby leg.

"How are you, Maya?" She asks. "You look so happy. But you need to rest. We won't stay for long."

Jagger agrees, "No, we won't keep you. Only a quick peek. You need your rest."

I chuckle to myself, thinking how alike my brother and I behave. He and Sage are couple goals.

"Congratulations, Little Sis, bro! You did it," Jagger says as he fist bumps with me. "Now, what do we call the little one officially?"

My face splits in two nearly as I wrap my arm around Maya's shoulders while I pat our pup's back. Maya turns him around to rest against her big boobs so he can face everyone. I hand my mobile to Jagger for him to take the video.

"Meet Ulf Larson!" I announce, beaming.

"Ulf! I love his name!" Exclaims Signy as she claps her hands. "It means wolf in old Norse."

"It sounds badass!" Dylan grins, his golden eyes twinkle with mischief.

My brother grips my shoulder and smiles. "Well done! A strong name for the newest addition to the Miami Wolves Pack. Tag and Wren had healthy pups. Today is a great day for our pack!"

I grin at my brother even as my wolf howls.

Time to claim my fated mate.

 *aya*

"Maya, you look incredible! I'm so happy for you and Viggo. Congratulations!"

Patricio pulls me into his arms as tears slip down my cheeks. It's so good to see my brother.

Viggo told me he had a surprise for me. We drove to The Larson Tower, with Ulf sleeping in my arms. I had no idea the surprise was Patricio.

It's been a couple of weeks since Ulf's birth. The next day, Viggo gave me a push present of an incredible blue diamond heart-shaped pendant on a delicate platinum chain. The heart aligns with mine to represent our little Ulf's heart beating in sync. I haven't taken it off since Viggo placed it around my neck. I treasure it but not nearly as much as I love Viggo and Ulf. They are my heart.

However, it beats quickly as my brother hugs me close. No more words pass between us. Yet we speak volumes.

Viggo stands to the side with Ulf held against his chest. I sense his watchful eyes on us. Even though he invited Patricio to Miami and we speak every week, Viggo remains leery. Not that I blame him.

It's been hard not having the support of my family all these months. Complete silence from my parents and Odalis. At first, I thought they would give in. I even called and sent text messages. But they went unanswered. I didn't tell Viggo, convinced he'd fly down to Caracas and have it out with them. After a while, I realized it's not worth it.

I chose to live my life as I pleased, and I will.

I dry my eyes and smile up at my brother. His handsome face lights up with a genuine smile full of love. My heart sings.

"Thank you, Patricio. I'm so happy you're here! Come sit. Do you want something to drink? Are you hungry?"

My mothering instincts expand beyond little Ulf. I find myself having the urge to care for others, too. Wren laughs and tells me I can come mother her triplets any day while she takes a much-needed nap. I join in her laughter knowing she'd have it no other way. Her trio of adorable wolf pups is her top priority, with Tag coming in a close fourth!

Natalie's pup is so sweet. He's bigger than the other four and not just because he's a few weeks older. She and

Rust say it's because they're born wolf shifters. It will be interesting to see if Ulf and Wren's pups differ. However, I don't worry about it. Ulf is bigger than a human baby. As with my pregnancy, he's at a more advanced stage at a younger age. So, I'm sure he'll keep up with everyone else.

Viggo says his pup is absolutely perfect. I agree!

Wren and I introduced them to the pack a week after we gave birth. We gathered in the clubhouse meeting space. It was so different from my first time standing before the pack. I wasn't nervous they wouldn't accept me. Or, if I'm honest, terrified they'd eat me. The she-wolves who made innuendos about their dalliances with Viggo oohed and ached over Ulf as much as they did the other newborns. The space vibrated with love. I couldn't be happier.

But not as happy as I am now as I sit beside my brother in a guest apartment. I realize Viggo had us come here to avoid Patricio visiting Moon Island. It's best to let him believe Viggo and I live here than to make him aware of the protected island.

Patricio turns to Viggo and opens his arms with a smile. "May I hold my nephew, Viggo?"

He hesitates, then crosses the distance between them. I can sense his need to protect our pup. I smile as he approaches. Our eyes meet, and I nod. He returns the gesture and places our pup in Patricio's arms. Viggo ensures my brother holds Ulf's head and cradles him to his chest. Viggo eyes Patricio as he holds him. Satisfied, he steps back and perches on the edge of the sofa beside me. I place a hand on his thigh and squeeze. He smiles while his gaze remains on our baby-pup.

"He's a handsome boy. The darkens of his hair combined with his pale blue eyes is striking. He'll be a charmer like his *Tío* Patricio!"

He chuckles and winks at Viggo. He doesn't crack a smile. My brother shakes his head and clears his throat. He glances between Viggo and me with serious eyes.

"Listen, I understand you're wary of our family, and I do not blame you in the least. They were wrong. I tell them every day," he says, then focuses on me. "Maya, you must live your life and not wait for our family to accept what happened. You know how stubborn *Papá* is, and *Mamá* follows right behind him. Odalis will do anything to please our father."

He flicks his gaze to Viggo and glances down at Ulf before he continues, "You have your family now. And of course, you will always have me. Do not allow ours to drain you of the joy you share with Viggo and Ulf. Focus on the gifts given to you. Do not miss out on a moment with them. Promise me, Maya."

I nod, too emotional to verbalize a response. Viggo strokes my back as he presses a kiss to my head. He murmurs comforting words for a moment before he faces my brother.

"Patricio, I appreciate your words. I'm sure it's difficult for you to go against your family to support Maya. They don't deserve either of you."

My brother inclines his head.

I take his words to heart. It's painful to know he's told them repeatedly how wrong they are. Yet I hear nothing from not one of them. It's foolish of me to hold back my life. I bring my gaze to Viggo and smile. I make my decision.

~

Viggo

I SENSE a change in Maya after her brother tells her to move on. My wolf grins with tongue lolling, convinced she decided to accept my claiming bite and to transition. To be one with me forever. I send a silent prayer to the gods my instinct is true. Then another one to get Patricio out of here and into his guest apartment. Not polite. But I don't give a damn. I want to be alone with Maya. Now.

Unfortunately, they spend hours talking. To make the time go faster, I go into the kitchen to prepare dinner. Maya's appetite increased since, as she told me, she burns loads of calories breastfeeding Ulf—and me. I can't get enough of her sweet milk.

I prepare one of her favorite dishes, shredded beef in a tomato sauce with roasted vegetables. The first time I made it and she smacked her lips, I teased she wanted it because it instinctively reminds Ulf of an animal his wolf hunted. She refused to eat the dish the second time, then asked me to cook it a week later. I chuckle to myself as I stir the red sauce.

My mind drifts to the other morning.

My enhanced hearing detected Ulf snuffling in the nursery while Maya slept peacefully. Wanting her to let rest, I decided to feed him from a bottle. Quietly, I slipped from the bed and left our suite. I strode with a purpose to his nursery. He waved his arms in the air, making sucking noises. A grin spread over my face as I crossed the room to his crib. With each step, my heart soared.

Who'd have thought the playboy prince of the pack focused on proving I'm my own male to be taken seriously would meet my fated mate at the club, fall madly in love, and have a pup?

Hell nah!

But here we are, and there I was picking up Ulf with a stinky diaper. I couldn't help but to chuckle at the irony. I'm ready for family life. Wow!

"Viggo? Did you hear me?"

I glance down at the sound of Maya's voice. She places a hand on my back and stares at me with questioning eyes.

Caught in my thoughts, I didn't detect her enter the kitchen. I smile and kiss the crown of her head.

"Sorry, my love. I didn't hear you. What did you say?"

She studies my face, then smiles.

"How's dinner going? Do you need any help?"

I glance over her head, looking for Ulf. Patricio stands by the island holding him. He smiles.

"I'm not handy in the kitchen. But I can pour the wine."

I realize I should give him a break. At least he attempts to be a part of Maya's life, and now Ulf's. I nod.

"Sounds good, thanks."

He walks over to Maya. She takes Ulf from his arms and sits at the island.

"The food smells delicious. What is it?" Patricio asks.

I offer him a taste as I tell him about Maya's favorite dish, leaving out the wolf shifter part. I smirk over my shoulder at her, and she grins.

"So, my tastes changed. I'll admit it."

We eat alfresco on the terrace with the panoramic view across Biscayne Bay, abuzz with water lovers, to the azure Atlantic Ocean. We fall into a companionable conversation through the meal to after-dinner drinks. The entire time, Ulf sleeps peacefully in his bassinet between Maya and me.

Patricio leaves with plans to spend the next day with Maya while I care for Ulf. We'll meet up again for dinner. It pleases me to see her eyes bright with happiness. No matter what happens with the rest of her family, she has her brother's love.

We bathe Ulf and settle him in his nursery for the night, then head to our suite. Maya slips her hand in mine and leans into me as we walk along the hallway. I bring our entwined fingers to my lips and kiss her knuckles as I inhale frangipani and coconuts. She sighs and smiles up at me.

"Viggo, make me yours in all ways, *Mi Amor*."

CHAPTER 18

aya

"Mmmmmm… Mmm mmm… Aaahhh!"

My eyes roll. My head flies back on my neck. I snap my legs together against the sides of Viggo's head. I jackknife off the bed. It's the third orgasm he's pulled from me since I awoke to his tongue laving my pussy. I'm incoherent at this point. My swollen pussy lips and engorged clit can't take any more of his licks, nips, and probes.

"Ooohh, Viggooo!" I wail as my body continues to convulse.

He growls his disapproval and nips my inner thigh. Then he adds two of his thick fingers to the mix. The strumming of my G-spot causes another orgasm to rise from the base of my spine.

I cry out from the unexpected sharp pain and toss my head from side to side. My bound wrists struggle against the silk belts attached to the ornate wooden headboard. Not only is Viggo my Viking warrior, he's resourceful. He made good use of the sumptuous robes in the en suite bathroom by repurposing the belts as restraints. I can only move my lower body fully and tug my arms fruitlessly.

"Bad girl," he admonishes as he parts my lower lips to spank my sensitive clit.

The moist sounds of flesh meeting flesh are a trigger for my body to respond with another mind-blowing climax. I mewl as it ignites my body in pure ecstasy.

"Be still, or I'll force you to cum five more times," Viggo threatens.

Ordinarily, that may sound like a phenomenal idea. But not after multiple rounds last night and this morning. I hate to admit it, but my body needs a break. He's determined to make my experience with his claiming bite a memorable one. And damn if it won't be. I'm so boneless, I'll never walk again!

"Viggooo… Please!" I beg.

Relief floods my system when he prowls up my body, leaving a trail of open mouth kisses on my heated skin. His ice blue eyes—now silver with lust—never leave mine. Hypnotized, I watch his approach. Only when I catch sight of his massive cock in my periphery do my eyes veer from his.

Viggo's dick is a sculpturesque piece of art. Hard as steel, covered in velvety soft skin. Veins and ridges stand in relief. The bulbous head reddened with need glistens with a drop of pre-cum on its slit. Its ten-inch length and girth too wide for my fingers to meet. His heavy balls swing at the base like a pendulum. The tantalizing sight makes my mouth water. I lick my lips. He chuckles.

"Hungry for what you see, my little wolf?" He asks as his voice thrums in my ear.

I nod and whimper my response.

He grips the base of his big dick and feeds the tip an inch inside of me.

I groan.

"Open up for me. I need to feel your tight pussy wrapped around me, milking my cock," he growls in a voice rough with desire.

Conditioned to respond to her mate, my body drains of the tension to allow him unrestrained entry. We groan together as he breaches my pussy lips. Once fully seated, Viggo stills. Entranced by the sensation of my pussy clenching around his pulsating cock, we don't utter a sound. Only the rapid beat of our hearts fills the air.

Not until my hips rise of their own accord demanding movement, does Viggo pull out to his tip then piston back inside of me. He wanted to give me the time I needed for my mind to catch up with my body in its appetite for more.

"Oh, baby... You feel so fucking good... So hot and wet..." Viggo grunts as his passion builds.

I writhe beneath him. My wrists pull against my restraints, aching to wrap my arms around his neck or grip his biceps for stability. Instead, all I can do is open and close my fists on air. He feels so good. So very good. But I need more.

Viggo takes one hand from my hip and places his thumb in my slack mouth. Without hesitation, I suckle it with fervor, pretending it's his dick. Once it's sopping wet, he pops it from my mouth and lifts me up onto his thighs as he sits back on his haunches.

Upright, he has more access to my body. His lips trail down the column of my neck to wrap around my fully aroused nipple. At the same time, he pulls my ass cheek to the side and presses the pad of his wet thumb against my puckered hole. My muscles in my pussy and ass tighten. He grunts from the strength of them on his dick.

"Aaahhh!" I scream as he plunders my bottom hole with his thumb and uses his muscular thighs to pump his cock up into my pussy.

My back arches and I keen with each bottoming out thrust. It seems as though I'll break in two from Viggo's power. An orgasm comes upon me with the speed of a freight train going downhill with no breaks. A bolt of lightning strikes me. Blinded with my body on fire, I ride Viggo like my life depends upon it.

"Fuuuck… Mayaaa!" He roars as my climax triggers his knot.

Inside of me, the base of his dick swells impossibly larger, locking us together. The tip presses against my womb. I cry out from the burn as it stretches my pussy.

Viggo bands one arm around my waist while the other hand sweeps my long hair to the side. It hangs over my shoulder. His flashing eyes stare into mine as his hand wraps around the back of my throat. I can't move.

He snarls and lowers his mouth to the juncture where my neck meets my shoulder. His hot breath blows across the sweaty skin. Warm liquid drips on the spot. Then pain sears me at the same time as hot ropes of his seed bathe my womb. Blood trickles down my shoulder. Liquid heat explodes in my pussy. I howl and struggle to break free of his hold.

Viggo's hand and arm tighten like bands of steel as his extended canines sink into my flesh. His mouth opens, then clamps back on the same spot. The serum from his canines lodges his scent under my skin to mark me as his permanently and to initiate my transition. He shakes his head to deepen the claiming bite.

Another wave crests over us as we continue to pound fiery flesh against fiery flesh in our frenzy to sate our carnal needs. When the last drop of Viggo's essence flows from his body to mine, we collapse breathless on the bed in a state of sheer euphoria.

"MINE!" He growls against my skin as he licks the bite.

It's the last thing I hear before darkness overtakes me.

～

Viggo

. . .

"You told me Maya's body needed to recover from the birth and to wait for six weeks before I issued my claiming bite. I did what you said. Now, five days have passed! How much longer do you think before she wakes up?!"

My gaze flicks between Rust and Natalie as we stand outside of Maya's room at Moon Island Hospital. I pray to the gods my worse fear doesn't happen. I cannot lose Maya. Especially since we have Ulf. Our pup needs his mother. I need my fated mate. Pain laces my heart at the thought she'll never wake up. *Do not take her from me!* I rail at the gods. My wolf howls mournfully.

"Viggo, we spoke with the other packs. The transition time ranges from four days to a week. It depends on the female," Rust says.

"Yes. I know it's difficult, Viggo. But have patience. Maya is a young, healthy, and fit female. I have no doubt she will recover. Give her body time to adjust. It's not a straightforward process to change the body's genetic makeup," Natalie adds as she rubs my arm.

"Why don't you come and sit, Viggo?"

I glance over at Wren, where she sits beside Maya's bed. She smiles reassuringly and holds out her hand. I flick my gaze to Jagger, Sage, and Signy where they stand with Tag, Dylan, and Sasha across the hall.

"I agree. She's connected to every machine possible to monitor her vitals. All is well. Go sit by your mate's side. Give her the comfort of your loving presence," Jagger says.

"Place Ulf on her chest like you did before. She responded well to him," Signy adds.

I listen to my siblings' advice and lift Ulf from his crib. I kiss the top of his head, covered with even more silky, jet black hair. He waves his arms as drool slips from his bow-shaped lips. I wipe it clean with a cloth and lay him on his mother's chest with my hand on his back.

I watch the two most important people in the world—my family. I send love down the mate bond formed when I issued my claiming bite. My heart, body, and soul beg Maya to open her eyes. A few minutes pass with no response. Only the steady pings of the machines sound in the room.

With a sigh, I lift Ulf from his mother's chest and cradle him against mine as I lower my cheek to his hair. I breathe in his pup scent of milk and soap while I murmur my love for him. With a heavy heart, I turn to place him in his crib.

"V—V—"

My heart stutters at the soft sound of Maya calling for me. I spin around to find her eyes fluttering open. She blinks against the light from the window and closes her eyes. Wren rushes to lower the shade, then leaves the room.

"Maya!" I exclaim.

My hand strokes her cheek as I call to her again. Slowly, she opens her eyes. I could drown in their topaz depths as she stares up at me. The corners of her lips curve.

"Viggo, Ulf," she says in a raspy voice. "Am I okay?"

A grin splits my face in two. I lean over and press my lips to hers. Fingers tangle in my hair as she pulls me closer and parts her lips. Our tongues twine on mutual groans.

Ulf babbles in my arms as though telling us enough. I lean my forehead on hers and chuckle.

"You're awake. Thank the gods."

"Viggo, let me check her."

I stand as Natalie closes the door and approaches the bed. She asks Maya questions as she examines her. I finally relax when Natalie confirms Maya is indeed okay, even better than the baseline tests she did before the transition. Pleased, Natalie leaves the room to tell the others.

"I can't believe I was out of it for so long. The whole time, I dreamed of a black wolf. Even now, I can see her in my mind's eye. Is that my wolf?" Maya says in between sips of water.

"Yes, and I will show you how to shift. After our mate bonding ceremony, we'll go to the Everglades camp for a pack run. My wolf can't wait to meet yours."

I turn at a knock on the door and call for them to enter. The gang troops in with whoops and words of congratulations. They gather around Maya, and she grins. She pats the bed beside her, and I sit, placing Ulf in her lap. She kisses his plump cheeks and cradles him in against her chest. With the other hand, she takes mine and kisses it.

"We're so glad to see you awake and strong, Maya," Jagger says, then glances at me before his gaze returns to her. "I know how eager Viggo is to complete your bonding. If you're up to it, the pack would like to celebrate your transition and witness your love with a mate bonding ceremony tonight. Would you like to do it?"

Tears stream down Maya's cheeks as she nods vigorously.

"That's so kind, thank you, Alpha."

Jagger beams at her use of his formal title as leader of our pack.

"Excellent! The Miami Wolves Pack will howl tonight!"

I grin as I brush Maya's tears with my thumb and press my forehead to hers.

"I love you, Maya Alejandra Larson."

"I love you, Viggo Larson."

A few hours later, as the sun sets, we stand before a ceremony bower of fragrant frangipani and jasmine flowers in the middle of Moon Island beneath the swaying fronds of palm trees. Their soft rustling seems to whisper words of joy at our union. The balmy air mixes with the floral aroma for a sultry scent. Whip-poor-wills chirp to welcome the night.

I wear a classic black tuxedo. But it's my smile with such jubilation in my heart that looks best. My fated mate returns my smile with one filled with love as she stands before me.

Signy helped her to select a crystal embellished evening gown with the sparkly stilettos that complement it so well. It hugs her round ass just the way I like it. Sage invoked a glamour spell to apply makeup and to put soft waves in Maya's hair. The tresses flow down her back, away from her radiant face.

We exchange our mate bonding vows with Ulf in my arms as we stand in front of our pack. My heart swells at how the members welcome Maya into our fold. They embrace her fully. Well, not the males or I'll tear their arms from their sockets…

After I slip a family heirloom princess-cut diamond and platinum ring on Maya's finger—the new pack princess—and she places a platinum band on mine, we face the others. The clearing at the center of Moon Island explodes with shouts and howls of elation.

I dip down and lift Maya onto my other arm. She giggles and wraps one arm around my neck while the other hand holds Ulf's hand. I throw my head back and howl. Maya joins in. I kiss her lips. Then, as a family, I carry them back up the aisle to wolf whistles and claps.

Maya is all mine. Forever.

CHAPTER 19

ix Months Later
Maya

"Come, my little wolf. Let's run in the moonlight as wolves."

My pussy quivers at Viggo's rich baritone as he takes my hand. We came to the pack's Everglades camp to celebrate the one-year anniversary of the first night we met. Wren and Tag pup-sit Ulf in their cabin nearby.

It's the place we go for pack runs and trainings. For generations, the virtually untouched area of the subtropical wilderness allows the pack the freedom to be in wolf form without prying eyes. Over the years, the original pack grounds grew from temporary cloth shelters to simple wooden cabins and now to luxurious residences scattered around the Alpha's house and clubhouse. Glamping—or glamorous camping—as Signy calls it. A few families and security members known as enforcers choose to remain here, not wanting the hustle and bustle of Miami for their principal home.

The camp sprawls out around us. Rather, the glamp since every cabin is a rustic mansion of logs and stones in various styles—some ranch and others multilevel, with and without front porches. They surround an open park-like square in the middle, where a lovely garden displays colorful flowers and bushes with wooden benches. Lanes crisscross the land to provide access to the various homes and structures.

A few pack members walk along or sit on porches. Their laughter and conversations fill the air. Cheerful smiles spread across their faces as they interact. The only surprising difference being some members in wolf form going about their business like it's an ordinary occurrence. Otherwise, the camp is an idyllic enclave with the spectacular Everglades as the setting.

Viggo leads me from our cabin and strides to the path lined by ornate wrought-iron lampposts. We walk in silence. He scans our surroundings while I absorb its beauty. The full moon illuminates the grassy areas where an abundance of trees rises to the night sky.

Raccoons scurry to the right. The little bandits lift their gazes from foraging to watch two lethal predators. They detect our wolves. Once we pass, the raccoons return to their dinner.

Rustling within the leaves of a nearby elm tree draws

my attention. I narrow my gaze to pinpoint the source. Red furry bodies extend wings. A colony of red bats awake from their slumber to hunt. Not a fan of the creatures, I turn my attention to the left.

Another grassy, tree-filled area stretches to a large pond. Its surface ripples with the breeze. Ducks huddle in nests gathered in bushes along its edge. Beaks appear from beneath their back feathers as they sense our wolves, too.

Viggo squeezes my hand, and I glance up at him. He tilts his chin towards a cluster of trees beyond the pond. I follow as he changes direction. When we reach the center hidden by low branches, he drops his black backpack to the grass.

"We'll shift here. You first. Our clothes will go in the backpack. Before I shift, I'll put it on. Remember to always stay by my side, Maya. Now, hand me your clothes and sneakers. Then shift."

My black wolf drops her front legs and raises her rear as her tail wags. She's ready to play, and so am I!

I peel off the t-shirt. My full breasts bounce free. The already puckered nipples tighten to peaks as the cool air licks at them. I toe off the sneakers. My hips shimmy as I slip out of the shorts. When I rise with the clothes bundled in my arms, Viggo stares at me. My cheeks flush crimson from his unleashed desire.

A needy whine rises in the back of my throat. He growls in response and stalks towards me. My clothes fall to the ground. Once again, he kisses me senseless. He pulls away, and my body leans towards him, drawn like a magnet to steel. Or rather to his velvet-covered steel rod that tents his shorts.

"I'm not waiting until we get back, little wolf."

I squeeze my thighs together as my fingernails dig into his forearms. *Ay Dios mío!* Does he mean to mount me in wolf form? My wolf leaps to her feet and howls.

"Shift, *mate.*"

His command catches me off guard, but not my wolf. She surges forward. Bones reshape and muscles lengthen as I shift to my black wolf. Amidst crackling and a flash, we stand on four legs moments later. My fur-covered head tilts back to gaze at him.

"So beautiful you are, Maya. Gorgeous," he murmurs as he circles me, trailing his fingertips along my neck and flank. The feathery edges of my tail slip through his fingers. They move to caress my spine and the top of my head.

He crouches in front of me and cups my jaw. "Now, I'll shift, and we'll run. Then mate."

My fur ripples as I shudder. *Yes!*

Viggo strips and adds his clothes with mine to the backpack. He loosens the straps, then loops his arms through. It hangs to the side. Moments later, it fits snug to his massive red wolf. The same wolf from my dreams. My fantasy lover come to life.

Slowly, I approach him with my head and tail low. My wolf wants to guarantee he sees we pose no threat. We are omega to his Alpha. I pause at a low growl. A tentative step forward elicits another low growl. Immediately, I drop to the ground and bare my throat and belly.

He pads forward and nuzzles my vulnerable areas. Hot breath blows my fur as he sniffs and chuffs.

I remain completely still.

He probes between my rear legs and rumbles. The flat of his textured tongue laves my sensitive bits.

I whimper.

He growls low in his throat.

A nip to my flank breaks my stillness. I yelp and gaze up at him. Tempered lust fills his eyes. He jerks his head, and I roll to all fours. A quick shake loosens the leaves and twigs stuck to my fur. He pads from beneath the branches. I follow.

We run and play through the sawgrass marshes and pine flatwoods. The scent of fresh grass, musky-sweetness of fallen leaves, squirrels asleep in their burrows, and unbathed humans flow through the crisp air past my nose. The pads of my feet snap twigs and grip boulders with every bounding step. My heart races as fast as my legs. Free!

Viggo slows and lopes towards a rock formation. He pauses outside the opening and blocks me from following. He steps inside. Seconds later, his head peeks out. He rumbles and steps back. I enter. My eyes dart around the cave.

Dirt covers the ground with windswept leaves scattered

about. The rough surface of the rocks creates three walls and a ceiling. Away from the evening chill, the temperature is comfortable—not that wolf shifters get cold. It's cozy.

Viggo prods me with his snout and shrugs his shoulders. I nod and use my teeth to tug the backpack straps from his body. I watch it drop to the ground. When my gaze lifts, he stares at me like a hungry predator ready to devour its prey.

~

Viggo

MAYA'S SCENT taunted my nostrils from the moment we stood outside our cabin. Many times, I had to fight the urge to push her against a tree and plunge my hungry cock deep into her cunt.

But I wanted to find a suitable place for us to mate as wolves for the first time. Now, I wish to take pleasure in her. My wolf howls in agreement.

I prowl towards her—a constant rumble in my chest. She remains still. I breathe in her unique scent as once again I nuzzle her neck, flank, and base of tail. With a possessive growl, I rise onto my hind legs and wrap my front ones around her waist and legs. My thighs bracket hers.

She lifts her tail.

I plunge my aching cock inside of her. She whines and stamps her front feet. I growl as my hips pump vigorously. Nips to her neck and shoulders still her wriggling. My knot expands. Her pussy contracts. She paws the ground, whining as we lock together. I rumble in my chest to soothe her while we remain carnally connected. I want another pup in her belly.

Fifteen minutes later, my knot deflates, and we separate. I nuzzle her flank and lick her snout. She returns my affection.

I step away and send my contented wolf back to the fringes of my being. He retreats at my will. On all fours, I stretch and watch as my beautiful mate shifts. I look forward to more times fucking her while we're wolves.

"Oh, Viggo," she purrs as she stretches. "That was amazing, *Mi Amor.*"

She presses her forehead against mine. A yawn interrupts our moment of bliss. She giggles and reaches for the backpack. Handing my clothes to me, she smiles.

"You wore me out, big bad wolf."

Kneeling, I chuckle and tug my t-shirt over my head. When we're dressed, I crawl out our den and scan the area. Maya crawls forward and slips her hand in mine. She stifles another yawn.

"Come. Let's get you home. I'll bathe you and tuck you in for a good night's sleep. I have surprises for you tomorrow."

She bounces on the balls of her feet and kisses my cheek.

Who expected I'd fall so hard for a fated mate I never knew existed a year ago?

And now I love her, our pup, and want another.

The pack prince met his match and more.

EPILOGUE

igny

"KEEP your head down and hold on, Signy! Hold on! Oh, gods—"

Across from me, the flight attendant shouts from her seat while the pilot and co-pilot attempt to regain control of my private jet.

It jounces in violent turbulence caused by an unexpected blizzard swept in from the Atlantic Ocean as we fly from Miami to New York. When I last glanced out the window, only thick swirls of snow appeared. The white fluffy clouds replaced by ominous gray ones until nothing was visible. I could see not even the wing or its flashing light.

I threw myself back against the plush leather seat and

tightened my seatbelt. I reached for my mobile in the seat next to me. But the jet dropped. The mobile flew from the seat and skittered across the floor. I cried out in horror as it crashed against the wall. The cracking of the screen let me know I had no means of calling for help. I couldn't reach my parents or my brothers in Miami. Nor anyone else in our pack. My wolf whined in despair.

The pilot announced they were going to circumvent the storm and reroute from the flight plan to JFK. The monitors showed a chance to avoid the worse of the storm if they flew further north of New York City.

Now, I wonder if anything would have made a difference as the jet banks left and drops several feet. The change in course is so severe, bile rises in my throat. I choke it down as I hold my head between my knees. Tears stream down my cheeks as I sob.

As a young she-wolf, I can survive most damage with my enhanced healing. Only silver can inflict fatal harm. But this? Flying miles up in the sky during a freak snowstorm that blocks visibility for the pilot and co-pilot? Not an easily recoverable situation should we crash.

My heart clenches at the thought. Please gods, no!

How can I go from poring over the latest edition of *Vogue* while listening to my favorite playlist to begging for my life? All I wanted was to go to New York Fashion Week as I do every season. Now, I wish I'd stayed at home.

All thoughts blow from my mind as the front of the jet dips. The seatbelt digs into my pelvis as I hang from the seat. My waist-length black hair covers my face like a curtain. A scream rips from my throat. It blends with the flight attendant's wail.

"We're going down! Brace yourselves!"

The pilot's terrified shouts make my blood run cold.

My ears pop as I scream. My hands reach out but flail with nothing to hold.

The jet jerks up enough for me to sit back with a gasp as my body pulls away from the seatbelt. I swipe my hair out of my eyes and swivel my head. The interior of the jet is a mess.

"Oh, fuck!"

The pilot curses as something drags along the bottom of the jet. Metal screeches, lights flicker, alarms sound. Cold air fills the cabin. Tendrils of smoke follow.

We have no time to react as the jet plummets.

The flight attendant and I stare in stark fear at one another.

My wolf throws herself to the ground. She reminds me to brace myself for impact. Arms lift to the sides of my head as I lower my chest to my knees. Fingers intertwine. I say a silent pray.

Then boom…

Cold. So very cold.

My trembling body wakes me. Every inch screams in pain. I black out.

"—way. Over here!"

"Holy shit! This is the worse crash I've ever seen."

"Where's the rest of it? Fuck…"

"Check her pulse. Is she breathing?"

Calloused fingers wrap around my wrist. Gently, they skim across the skin. A jolt of electricity zips from the touch and up my arm. I cry out.

"She's alive!"

"Thank the gods."

"What about the others?"

No!!! Please let them be alive, too.

Another jolt—but not a pleasurable one—courses through me as I try to sit up.

"Do not move."

Something warm infused with the enticing scents of sandalwood and vanilla covers me. Stubble scratches my neck. A deep inhalation against my skin makes me shudder. I cry out in a combination of ecstasy and agony. The man hisses. He jerks away.

"No, fucking way," he mutters.

"Do you smell that?"

"She can't be."

Who are these men?

My eyelids hurt as they flutter open. Blurry images in the shapes of three enormous men appear in the darkness. I blink to clear my vision, then reopen my eyes.

Glacial blue ones stare down at me. I watch mesmerized as they darken to cobalt, then flash electric.

The other two men snarl and growl. Surprised, my gaze shifts to them.

But a rumble draws my attention to the first man's face.

The air leaves my lungs as my mouth falls slack.

Jet black hair frames chiseled cheekbones and firm jaw.

The silky strands hang to his bulging pecs. Muscular arms fold across his broad chest, covered in only a white tank top. On top of it, dog tags hang from a chain-link and leather necklace. My gaze follows the chain up to his magnificent face.

He studies me with an intensity that makes me tremble, and not from the cold.

THANK you for reading *Viggo The Obsession*!

If you enjoyed the book, I would so appreciate your review as they make a huge difference for indie authors. Be sure to sign up for my newsletter for the latest info about the series, new releases, and a FREE book at **bit.ly/ CLBooksDylanTheRogue**! Want more of Signy's story? Read *Signy's Mates: A Wolf Shifter Fated Mates Reverse Harem Romance*. Turn the page for a preview of *Jagger The Temptation* and Signy.

PREVIEW JAGGER THE TEMPTATION: A WOLF SHIFTER FATED MATES PARANORMAL ROMANCE

Jagger

"THE QUARTERLY NUMBERS show an increase in profits. More than projected because of the opening of the beach-front resort in Charleston earlier than planned. The general manager reports the property sold out for the first four months..."

I nod as my Vice President of Hotels and Resorts for Larson Enterprises, Inc. continues his update. My mind focuses partially on his presentation.

For the last few weeks, I can't seem to focus. I don't know whether lack of sleep causes the lapse or something else. Dreams of another dominate my nights. They remain just out of reach, on the fringes. But it's their silent pleas for help that keep me tossing. A vibration from them of fear and sadness draws me closer. My instinct kicks in, and I want to save them, protect them.

Each dream brings me closer to them. But they remain just out of reach. I wake tangled in silk sheets. An arm extended as my hand reaches for them. Last night I called a name. However, as the last vestiges of the dream slipped away, the name dissolved with it.

I growl low in my chest in frustration.

My COO shifts his gaze to me. His wolf senses picked up my displeasure with ease.

I shake my head at Tag Dahl.

He cocks his head at me.

As my best friend, he's known me since we were pups. Born within a few weeks of each other—him to our pack's enforcer and me to our Alpha—Tag knows me as well as I know myself. I haven't mentioned my dreams to him, not that he'd think me nuts. No. I just don't know what they mean and if they warrant a conversation for analysis.

And Tag would delve into their meaning.

As my beta, he's my right-hand man. Anything that involves me and can impact our pack, he wants to solve the puzzle.

But this one will remain under wraps until I figure it out. So, I shake my head again and turn my attention back to the presentation. Even as I will my mind to pay full attention. I remove my personal hat. Then I firmly affix the one for my roles as CEO and Chairman of the Board of the luxury hotels, fine dining, clubs, and lounges company my family founded in Miami.

An hour later, a persistent Tag strides along with me to my suite of offices in The Larson Tower on Biscayne Bay. We pass through the executive floor as staff—wolf shifter and human—acknowledge us. The unaware humans often stare in awe at our formidable sizes. We're both six feet, seven inches of pure muscle and move with predatory grace. We nod in return but continue without pause.

I know Tag wants to find out what's up with me. I'll allow his henpecking since we're so close. Otherwise, I do not tolerate others in my business. No. One.

"Alpha, you have a few voicemails, sir."

"Thanks, Ginny," I respond to my administrative assistant as I open the double doors of my office. "Kindly hold my calls."

"What's up, Jagger?"

I bite back an irritated growl—lack of sleep will have you pissed, even at your best friend who only wants to help.

"You want a drink?" I ask as I unbutton the jacket of my bespoke three-piece Brioni suit and stride to the bar cart. It's after five-thirty, and I can use a stiff one before I head out to Club Sol & Mani for some much-needed sexual relief.

"Sure, thanks."

I take my time pouring two fingers of scotch into the Baccarat crystal tumblers. Absolutely no rush to have Tag pick at my psyche. My ears pick up his almost silent huff, and I chuckle to myself.

"Don't delay this conversation, Jag. You've been off for a few weeks now, and I've given you space," he says, then nods his thanks for the liquor. "What's up with you?"

Again, I allow him to question me, even though I'm his Alpha and my word is final.

I lower myself onto the dove gray tufted leather sofa in the seating area. Tag takes a chair opposite and places an ankle over a knee. I sip my drink as I consider my words. He knows better than to interrupt at this point.

"Dreams."

He cocks his head at the simple one-worded response. I shrug and take another sip.

"For the past few weeks, dreams invade my sleep. Every. Single. Night. Someone's in trouble. But I can't catch their name or where they are to help them," I sigh and stare out the window.

The panoramic view across Biscayne Bay with jet skiers and megayachts on its dazzling surface out to the azure Atlantic Ocean helps to quiet the inner turmoil my wolf and I sense. He turns his massive silvery white head to stare at me with accusatory ice blue eyes. It's as though he knows something I don't and pissed I'm not aware. I run my fingers through my white blond hair as I think on it, then shake my head. No clue.

"What do you recall?" Tag asks as he leans forward and places his elbows on his knees, the scotch tumbler balanced between his sizable hands.

I shrug.

"A brightness in the background prevents a clear view. I know it's outdoors since I hear the hum of insects and feel the warm sun on my skin. Naked skin. So, I must have shifted and returned to my human form."

Another sip of scotch, and I stand to pace my office.

Instinct tells me these are no ordinary dreams. But each morning I account for the whereabouts of my pack, and no one turns up missing. Not knowing who calls for my help drives me and my wolf mad.

I growl and toss back the rest of my scotch. A few long strides and I refill the tumbler.

"No one in our pack seems in trouble. I'll stop by the she-wolves' residences on my way home just to make sure. A few of our unmated males flew to New Orleans for the weekend. I'll shoot a text to them and make sure they didn't get into anything on Bourbon Street."

With a nod of agreement, I hold the decanter up. Tag declines a refill—ever the responsible one. Fine. It's not like wolf shifters can get drunk. Well, not too much. Our systems process substances differently from humans. All the better for us, especially when I'm in this pissy mood.

"Well, you know they say fated mates can have dreams about the other. The more frequent and intense they become, the closer the pair gets to their first encounter," Tag says. His emerald green eyes scan my face for a reaction. He knows I've waited all these years for my fated mate—and will continue to do so.

Despite my father's damn near daily persistence, I issue

the claiming bite and complete the mating bond with a single she-wolf. The last eleven years of nearly nonstop mating runs, with the she-wolves in my pack and those from nearby cities—hell, even overseas. Or galas at our hotels and mixers at our clubs, an accidental encounter, all to persuade me to select a she-wolf as my mate. None of them tempt me in the slightest.

All the she-wolves desire to bond with me. Then the supposed prince—and they were eager to lose their slippers and thongs for me to pick up——now the Alpha of the Miami Wolves Pack. Correction, *Billionaire Wolves of Miami* as the other packs refer to us. With good reason, since we're the most powerful pack in the South.

Several millennia ago, Scandinavian Viking wolf shifters sailed from the Old World and landed along the East Coast of what's now the United States. The six packs headed by best friends who sought new lands moved throughout the continent to form territories with ours settling here. We maintain close ties with our brethren through friendship, mating, and business. Plus, our Ruling Council gatherings keep us informed of happenings throughout the packs.

And even going that far and wide, I have yet to meet my fated mate. However, I will wait for her.

Hell, my wolf demands it as he gets agitated when he senses a she-wolf's burgeoning interest. Sure, he'll sit back while I fuck since it fills a need and doesn't equate to being mated. Wolf shifters—male and female—have strong sexual appetites. We don't have the same hang-ups as humans over casual sex, no sex before marriage, and whatever other bullshit they come up with. It's a part of our lives, just like eating or breathing. A need we won't suppress. Particularly with the built-up tension raging through my body. However, his pacing and snarls have increased recently, too.

So maybe Tag is on to something.

My *fated* mate.

A she-wolf whose scent I was born with teasing my nostrils. When she appears, I will recognize her by her distinct scent. No other will bear her uniqueness. Someday we will meet. I will give her my claiming bite, and we will have our mate bonding ceremony for all the clans to witness. I will make her mine forever.

The thought she may be in trouble makes my blood boil and my wolf snap his teeth, ears flat to his head. Our protective instinct on high alert.

So, I won't give up on finding my fated mate—or on us. No matter how many times my father bugs me about the need to bond with another. I'm no longer the teen who had to obey.

I am Alpha now.

"WE'RE HERE, ALPHA."

I glance up from my mobile screen and out the tinted window.

So focused on business emails, I didn't notice my driver

pull my Black Badge Rolls-Royce Cullinan into the driveway for Club Sol & Mani Miami. The flagship of six exclusive, luxury, members only BDSM clubs Larson Enterprises owns sits on Ocean Drive directly across from the Atlantic Ocean in a South Beach historic, beachfront gated mansion.

"Great, thank you, Cole," I respond. "I'll take it from here and will text when I'm ready to go home."

"Yes, Alpha. I'll get the door for you."

I wave him off and reach for the handle, only for the club's valet to open the door. A nod to Cole and a thanks in the form of a hundred to the young wolf shifter, and I stride to the scrolled wrought-iron and glass doors of the Spanish-style mansion. Laughter from members as they frolic in the mosaic-tiled pool within the sun-filled courtyard floats in the balmy evening air.

"Good evening, Alpha," the doorman says with a respectful bow of his head. I shake his hand and palm off another hundred. He thanks me as I move on.

"Hello, Alpha!" The two she-wolf greeters chorus cheerfully as I walk through the opulent lobby to the elevators. Another two C-notes and I'm on the elevator headed to my personal suite.

Tonight, I'll play in privacy rather than amongst other members in Exhibition where demonstrations and performance rooms provide entertainment—or inspiration. Nor will the Dungeon do, despite my affinity for the spacious section devoted to public forms of BDSM play. Those not in the lifestyle may think it's a medieval dungeon for torture with the St. Andrew's Crosses, spanking benches, chains suspended from the ceiling, and more. To me, the pieces and assorted whips, floggers, canes, and implements are only to be expected.

The soft thrum of sensual music greets me as I step out of the elevator and into the hallway. The rhythm vibrates through my core as intended to amp arousal for what lies behind the closed doors of the eight private suites. Members can reserve them in advance should they prefer the same privacy I wish for tonight.

Each suite decorated by theme has various BDSM pieces, implements, and toys. A nice variety of options to choose from. However, my suite remains for my personal use only.

I press my palm against the plate by the door of the corner suite, and the locks disengage.

"Good evening, Alpha."

My head jerks up. What the fuck?! I allow no one in my space without my consent. My ice blue eyes adjust to the candlelit room. On my custom-built mahogany wood, king-size bed cornered by four thick carved posters and a brass lattice canopy with rings strategically attached sits a she-wolf from my pack. And not just any she-wolf. The sable-haired hellion.

"Melissa, what the fuck are you doing in my suite?!" I snarl as I stalk towards her.

She jerks back as though slapped but recovers quickly. Fully naked, she rises from the bed with the prowess of a wolf in hunt mode and slinks towards me. Amber eyes glow in the candlelight. She tosses her waist-length sable brown hair over her shoulders. Her sleek figure with high perky tits tipped by puckered rosy nipples, flat belly, narrow waist, slim hips, and long, toned legs would make any male salivate.

Not me.

Even though I planned to fuck her tonight—after I *invited* her to my suite—my stomach churns at the thought as my wolf growls low in his broad chest. He's not happy, nor am I.

Melissa is one of my regular sexual partners. We scratch the itch for each other from time to time. However, it's not like we're exclusive. Many a she-wolf join me for carnal pleasures. As Melissa has with other males. And I've made it clear I am not interested in bonding with her.

But after this stunt, this may very well be the last time I hookup with her. If she thinks she can enter my domain uninvited, she's confused. And I will speak with the club manager about her gaining unapproved access.

I have no intention of giving Melissa any ideas.

Not happening.

For one, Melissa thinks she's the alpha since the other male wolf shifters in our pack bow down to her beauty and succumb to her whims. I won't have it.

Not to mention she's a bully. Another trait I will not tolerate. I treat everyone in our pack with respect. They may not be my equal, but I don't make them feel less than.

And the most important reason… She's not my fated

mate. The only wolf shifter who will enter my domain as she pleases.

My wolf agrees with a flick of his feathery tail.

"Melissa, I have told you we fuck. Nothing more"—I raise my hand to stop her response—"You have no right to enter my personal suite without my permission. None. Get dressed. I will inform the club manager not to allow you entry ever again. This is it. Do you understand?"

She blinks, then her mouth opens.

I fold my arms over my chest and stand with feet spread far apart in a dominant manner as I pin her with an arctic gaze.

Naturally, Melissa glares back and mimics my stance as her eyes blaze golden fire.

"Jag—"

"Alpha! Alpha, Melissa. And do not forget it. We may have fucked. But you will respect me as your Alpha. Get. Dressed. And. Go. Now."

She lifts her chin in defiance, then reconsiders when I slap my sizable palm on my muscular thigh. Her eyes widen at the warning. Then she scurries to the chair and gathers her clothes to her flushed chest.

"Yes, Alpha!" She exclaims.

With a stern eye, I watch as she dresses quickly.

Melissa stops at the door and glances at me over her shoulder. Her oval-shaped face pinched with worry. She knows she took it too far this time.

"Sorry, Alpha," she whispers, then opens the door and leaves.

I sigh and sink onto the bed.

Well, there goes the idea of releasing tension. More just built up.

With his tongue hanging out from the side of his mouth, my wolf yips. Ice blue eyes gleam with mirth. It's as though he laughs at my misfortune.

I growl at him and slump back on the navy blue silk pillows. My thoughts drift to my conversation with Tag. Perhaps fate doesn't want me with another since my mate will appear soon. My eyes close on a sigh.

Where are you?

Click the Image Below or Visit books2read.com/u/ mZEL2e For Your Copy

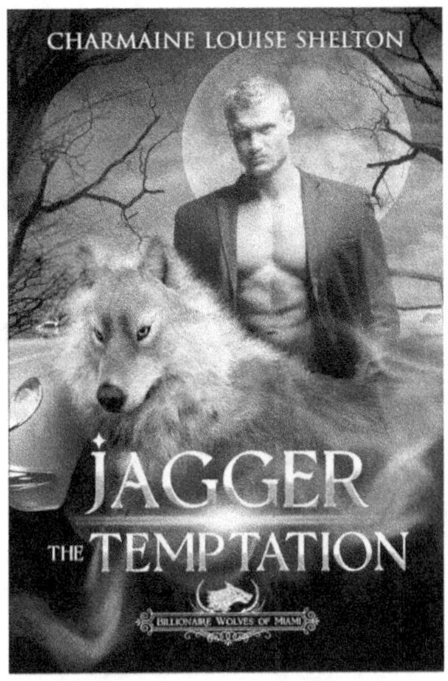

Jagger The Temptation: A Wolf Shifter Fated Mates
Paranormal Romance

NEXT IN SERIES SIGNY'S MATES:
A WOLF SHIFTER FATED MATES
REVERSE HAREM ROMANCE

What happens when I suffer amnesia and three powerful wolf shifters rescue me from a plane crash?

I open my eyes and lose more than my precious mind to the gorgeous males of the Billionaire Wolves of New York. Snowbound and unrecognizable, they offer me shelter and time to heal. Even though I can't remember my past, my future promises just what I need to find love.

But Garrett, the pack leader, Dolph, his second, and Colin, the enforcer, share secrets with their special ops missions that put me in danger.

When they learn I'm Signy Larson the pack princess of Miami, they want to claim me as their fated mates queen and keep me in their fortress forever.

But will my family allow it? Better yet, will I?

Read **Signy's Mates** today.

Their steamy love story is a standalone in the sizzling Billionaire Wolves Series of interconnecting stories featuring wolf shifter fated mates romance. Get a glimpse of their dynamism in other books.

Click the Image Below or Visit books2read.com/u/ 4ARKLp For Your Copy

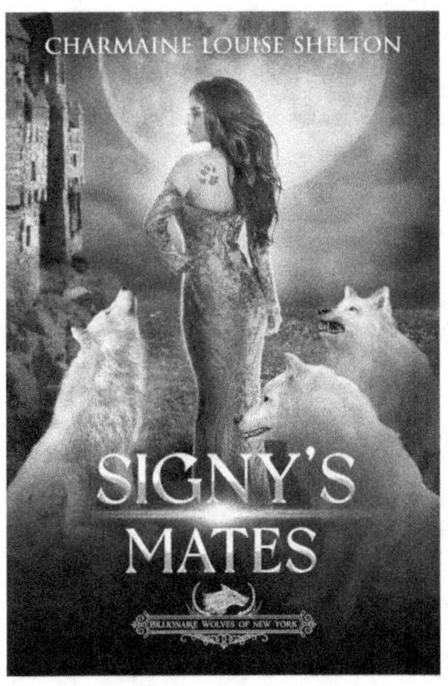

Signy's Mates: A Wolf Shifter Fated Mates Reverse Harem Romance

WANT FREE BOOKS?

Want to know what happened to Jagger's best friend Dylan? Find out in *Dylan The Rogue: A Wolf Shifter Fated Mates Paranormal Romance* your FREE Book!

Click Cover Below or visit **bit.ly/ CLBooksDylanTheRogue** to subscribe to my newsletter for latest news and launches, books from my author friends, and sizzling reads in book promotions. Plus, start reading the steamy fated mates romance for bad boy wolf shifter Dylan.

FREE BOOK!

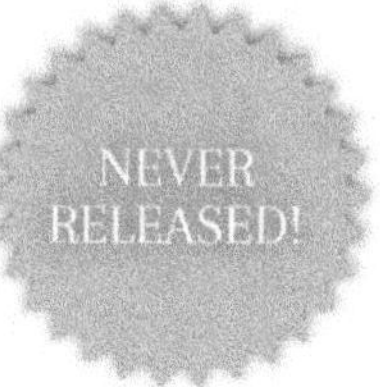

EXCLUSIVE FOR SUBSCRIBERS!

A Trilogy of Desires Roger & Leonie Parts I-III

Series Extras

Series Playlist

STEELE INTERNATIONAL, INC. - JACKSON
CORPORATION

A BILLIONAIRES ROMANCE SERIES CROSSOVER

Tempt My Desires Lachlan & Haley Part I

Tease My Desires Lachlan & Haley Part I

Grant My Desires Lachlan & Haley Part III

JACKSON CORPORATION

A BILLIONAIRES ROMANCE SERIES

Evoke My Desires Laurent & Yessenia Prequel

Light My Desires Laurent & Yessenia Part I

BILLIONAIRE WOLVES SERIES

WOLF SHIFTER FATED MATES PARANORMAL ROMANCE

MIAMI

Jagger The Awakening

(Available Exclusively for a Limited Time in Lunar Rising: A
Collection of Paranormal Romance)

Dylan The Rogue

(Available Exclusively to Subscribers)

Jagger The Temptation

Rust The Rejected

Tag The Redemption

Viggo The Obsession

ABOUT CHARMAINE LOUISE SHELTON

Charmaine Louise Shelton loves a dominant Alpha hero—human, shifter, or vampire—as long as he's a billionaire and sexy as sin! Her romance novels take readers into the heroes' glitzy, glamorous, steamy worlds as they chase after independent women who unexpectedly capture their hearts. Want to experience some more? Download a free book at CharmaineLouiseBooks.com!

Find her at:
CharmaineLouiseBooks.com

Follow her on social media on your favorite channels below and **download your Free Book** at CharmaineLouise Books.com.

Fulfill Your Desires.

DEDICATION

To my awesome and dedicated beta readers and ARC Team, my amazing author friends, and this incredible community for their support.

And most of all to you, my loyal readers who love these couples as much as I do.

Thank you!

Cover Design: Murphy Wallace, Midnight Designs

Fulfill Your Desires.

xoxo
Charmaine Louise Shelton

www.ingramcontent.com/pod-product-compliance
Lightning Source LLC
Chambersburg PA
CBHW070453200726

48293CB00007B/2187